# Madness

HAVE YOU BEEN CALLED?

START YOUR TRAINING AT

WWW.SOTERIANS.COM

book four THE SOTERIANS SERIES

# Madness

JACQUELYN WHEELER

*For Dad*

"Be loving enough to absorb evil and understanding enough to turn an enemy into a friend."
~ Martin Luther King, Jr.

## About the Soterians

Soteria was the ancient Greek goddess of safety and deliverance. When the balance of good and evil tips too far in evil's favor, certain worthy people carrying a rare gene develop special powers and are called forward to restore the balance. These people are known as *Soterians*. Once they have restored the proper balance of good over evil, their powers fade, and they resume their normal lives. There are five primary types of Soterians: Scouts, Empaths, Sentries, Warriors, and Mentors.

*Scouts* are responsible for reconnaissance, which allows the unit to make targeted moves and minimize risk and damage on both sides. Scouts have very acute vision and hearing, can become invisible, and can fly.

*Empaths* are the healers and illusionists of a unit. They can read other people's feelings, cast illusions, and heal allies.

*Sentries* are the defenders of their unit. Their extraordinary strength allows them to be a physical barrier to harm and can stop an enemy in his tracks. They protect themselves and their allies by emanating a shield that bullets, fire, and gas cannot penetrate.

*Warriors* go on the offensive and take down the enemy when all else fails. Their incredible speed and strength make them highly valuable.

*Mentors* find and train Soterians. They have the ability to tap into universal knowledge in times of crisis.

When conditions are right, Deimos, the ancient god of fear and the greatest source of evil on earth, rises out of hibernation and spreads evil across the globe. When this happens, a Soterian with a special combination of talents can evolve into an *Alchemist*. An Alchemist draws power from both good and evil and has all of the other Soterians' powers, as well as the ability to generate fire, making Alchemists the most powerful and most dangerous of all the Soterians. Alchemists are very rare.

Lastly, *Keepers* are not Soterians but are trusted allies of a unit and help with their missions. They play an important role in doing research and assisting the entire unit.

The Soterians series is about modern-day Soterians told through the eyes of Ashlyn Woods, a Scout and an Alchemist. *Madness* is the fourth book in the series.

| *Santa Barbara Unit* | *San Francisco Unit* |
|---|---|
| Mentor: John Gordon | Mentor: Theresa Silva |
| Scout: Ashlyn Woods | Scout: Jesse Burton |
| Empath: Rebecca Epstein | Empath: Claire Marks |
| Sentry: Christoph Voight | Sentry: Kenji Fukawa |
| Warrior: Michael MacNeil | Warrior: Raina Forrester |
| Keeper: Kai Anderson | Keeper: Paul Adams |

# Table of Contents

## Chapter One: Old Flames

"Ready?" I asked.

"Yeah, let's go." Kai picked up his guitar and headed for the door.

"Mom, we'll be back late," I called up the stairs. "Don't wait up."

She leaned over the banister, her blonde hair falling across her pretty face. "Ashlyn, for heaven's sake, I didn't wait up even when you lived here. Good luck, Kai. Hope it goes great tonight." She gave him a proud smile. From mom's perspective, Kai was already her son-in-law, even if I wasn't ready to take the long walk down the aisle yet.

We drove over the Bay Bridge into San Francisco and, amazingly, found parking within walking distance of the club. We had plenty of time, but Kai was striding quickly along the sidewalk.

"If you're in a hurry, I could fly us there," I offered as I jogged to keep up with him. "Say the word and we'll be invisible."

"No, we're almost there. Save your powers for dealing with Maggie."

"Seriously. She didn't call me once after I moved to Santa Barbara, and now a year later she's suddenly decided I'm her best friend again? Couldn't *possibly* have anything to do with my connection with you guys."

"Maybe she's coming to see Hollow Ground. We're just the opening act."

"I doubt it," I snorted. "All she can talk about is Waterfall. Not that you're not an amazing band, of course. I just don't trust her motives."

We arrived at the club, where we found Michael standing by the front door with a highly irritated expression on his face. He looked incredibly hot, as always, and I saw Kai glance at me with a small smile. I ignored the look and took Kai's hand as we approached.

"Hey, Michael. Where's Marlowe?"

"Backstage. She's doing her warm-ups or something."

Kai nodded. "She always does that. Vocal exercises and meditation before every gig."

"She said I'd be a distraction," Michael growled. "She told me to wait outside."

I bit my lip to keep from laughing. Powerful Warriors like Michael weren't used to being kept out of places they wanted to go. But Marlowe had pretty much turned his life upside down.

"Come on," I suggested. "I'll go in with you and we'll find a table. Kai likes to spend about six hours tuning and setting up his gear anyway." I put my arms around him, lacing my fingers through the soft curls at the back of his neck. "Have a great gig, okay? I love you."

"I love you, too," he said and kissed me deeply. "See you after the show." He gave my hand another squeeze and went inside. I turned to Michael.

11

"It's too bad none of the San Francisco unit could make it to the show. Lousy timing for them to all be training in the mountains this weekend. Any word from John? Or are we actually going to get a whole night off from fighting evil?"

Michael shook his head. "It's been nothing but nights off lately."

"Maybe for you," I said, looking around.

"You think you're going to find Deimos just walking down the street in the middle of San Francisco? Or maybe you think he's coming to Kai's gig."

"Laugh all you like, but I wouldn't put it past him."

"Why? You don't even know who he is."

"That's exactly the problem, which I intend to solve as soon as possible. Be quiet so I can concentrate." I reached out with my feelings, but as usual, I couldn't pick up anything that felt like it might be coming from the ultimate source of evil. I kicked the ground in frustration. The truth was, since we'd completed our last mission, I'd become somewhat obsessed with finding Deimos. I had been so sure that he'd been the man who had almost succeeded in killing me, that even though I thought I was about to die, I actually felt relief that we'd finally figured out who he was. Since then, I'd dreamed about him almost every night. Clearly, it was time to find out who he was so we could get to work figuring out how to stop him. The problem was that he could be anyone, and our only hope was that as an Alchemist, I might have the power to detect his presence. But right then, all I could detect was some weird bubbly energy aimed toward me . . .

"Ashlyn? Omigod, there you are!" I turned to see Maggie prancing toward me. She flicked her cigarette into the gutter and threw her arms around me, the smell of tobacco mingling with the scent of her strawberry shampoo.

"Hey, Maggie! I'm so glad you could make it."

"I can't believe they got a last-minute show right here in San Francisco!" she said, her eyes shining. "I mean, I just *love* these guys. Especially that hot guitar player of yours. How did you meet him again?"

"Kind of a long story," I said, taking a step back. "Maggie, this is Michael, one of my friends from Santa Barbara. Michael, this is my friend Maggie. She and I grew up together in Berkeley."

"Hi, Michael," Maggie said, looking him up and down admiringly. Michael just nodded in reply, his mind clearly elsewhere.

"So, you want to go in and stake out a spot?" I asked.

"Sure, let's just wait another minute for Todd. He's looking for parking."

It took me a few seconds for my brain to catch up with what she had just said. "Todd? You don't mean *that* Todd?"

"Oh yeah! Didn't I tell you? He offered to be designated driver, so who was I to argue? Oh good, here he comes now."

Sure enough, my ex-boyfriend Todd was walking toward us with his typical swagger and that stupid smile he always wore when he thought he'd done something especially clever.

"Hey, Ash, how's it going?" he asked as he put his arm around Maggie.

"Let's go in and get a drink," Maggie said brightly.

I resisted the urge to rub my temples as I felt Todd's smug sense of victory, Maggie's empty-headed enthusiasm, and Michael's amusement all blended together in one irritating jumble. This obviously wasn't going to be my night.

"So what have you been up to?" I asked Maggie when we were settled inside the club. It was already starting to fill up with people, most of whom were quintessential San Francisco hipsters wearing all kinds of fascinating facial hair designs and several piercings. One girl even had a diamond stud in her throat, which I found both really cool and kind of queasy-making at the same time.

"Tons of stuff!" Maggie gushed. "I saw Whitebox play last week, and get this: I actually got to go back stage! It was *amazing*." As she went on and on about the autographs she'd gotten, I glanced over at Michael. He was watching me with a curious expression on his face. I got a vague sense that he was trying to reconcile the Ashlyn he knew with the person I used to be.

"Well, I'm getting another beer," Todd said. "Ash, can I get you one?"

"You know I don't drink, and don't call me Ash. Besides, I thought you were designated driver."

"That doesn't mean I can't drink *anything*," he said. "Michael, how about you?"

"I don't drink, either."

"No shit?" Maggie looked astonished. "I think you two are the only non-drinkers I know. Not that there's anything wrong with it. In fact, it's really cool," she said, giving Michael a sultry smile. "Oh look, there they are!"

We turned to see Kai, Ryan, and Max walk out on stage and start setting up their gear.

"Where's the singer?" Todd asked. "I hear she's got a great ass."

I felt Michael stiffen next to me. I touched him on the elbow and sent healing into him to calm him down.

"Kai is soooo gorgeous," Maggie said as she watched him bend over to plug in his amp. "Does he do martial arts with you?"

"Yeah," I said through gritted teeth. Michael touched me on the elbow and then chuckled to himself. I tried to ignore him. My irritation was already reaching dangerous levels.

"What kind of martial arts?" Todd asked.

"We do a variety of styles," Michael answered. "Essentially a combo of Karate, Judo, and Aikido."

"More like *hot*-kido," Maggie said in a smarmy voice as she stared at Kai. I felt an almost uncontrollable urge to slap her.

Todd went to get more drinks as the band started warming up. I tried to just focus on Kai, but Maggie kept asking me questions and blathering on about people I didn't know or care about.

Finally, the band started playing, and Marlowe walked out on stage. She looked absolutely stunning, as always. She was wearing a blood-red corset tucked into a black leather mini skirt trimmed with chains and lace. Despite the very high heels of her boots, she moved with a grace that always made me feel like a troll.

As she grabbed the microphone and started singing, I heard Michael's heart pounding. I glanced at him and marveled at the intensity of his gaze as he stared at Marlowe.

"Someone's getting lucky tonight," Maggie said with a grin and looked significantly at Michael.

"Hey, not bad," Todd said as he walked up and put two beers down on the table. "Oh man, would I like to get a piece of that."

Michael jumped to his feet, but before he could make a move, I grabbed his arm. "Good idea, let's dance!" I said and jerked him toward the stage.

"You actually dated that asshole?" Michael spat.

"Please don't remind me," I said, weaving us through the crowd. "Anyway, you can't fight them all, Michael. And Marlowe can take care of herself."

"I can't stand thinking of her having to deal with people like him."

15

"Well, get used to it." I stopped halfway to the stage and turned to Michael. "We just have to learn to let go. This is their calling, and we have to support them, no matter what."

He looked around. "I guess I hadn't really thought about the fans. And the worst part is that not all of them are assholes."

I laughed. "Do you honestly think Marlowe is going to run off with someone else?" But I stopped laughing when I saw his face, which was wracked with pain. "Jesus, you and I have more in common than I thought. Listen, I've felt what's in Marlowe's heart, and in Kai's. They are both completely devoted to us. They're going to be fine. And so are we."

"Yeah, but . . . "

"Shut up and dance already." I turned toward the stage and danced to the next few songs, losing myself in their intoxicating sound. Their music made me feel like I was flying, and I had to work hard to keep myself from floating above the floor.

Suddenly, I felt an irritating sensation, and I turned to see Maggie and Todd dancing next to me. I turned and noticed that Michael had disappeared, which was all for the best. I was starting to get really angry. Why had Maggie insisted on befriending me again? Why had Todd come with her to the show? Why couldn't I just enjoy seeing the band in peace?

"Yeah! Shake it!" Todd yelled. He was watching Marlowe dance on the stage, nodding his head to the music and staring at her with a stupid smile.

"Whoooo!" Maggie screamed as Kai launched into a blistering solo.

"I see why they're called Waterfall," Todd said. "She's got sex flowing off her like water."

I felt the heat rising to my face. "They didn't name themselves after her," I retorted.

16

"Sure they did. Just look at her."

"No, they didn't. That's Kai's nickname for *me*."

Todd looked at me condescendingly. "Well, that's what he told you, anyway."

"What are you saying? That he lied to me?"

"Ash, don't get so worked up. I'm sure he was just trying to make you feel better." He looked back at Marlowe. "It's gotta be hard to know that those two are off touring together. No way is he going to be able to keep his hands off her."

I stared straight ahead, trying to stay calm. I could feel fear and anger and frustration and jealous rage all welling up inside me. "Todd, if you know what's good for you, you'll just shut the hell up."

"I know what's good for *you*, anyway." He slipped his arm around my waist.

Something inside me roared to life.

A volcano of emotion surged up from my core, and a second later, Kai's amp exploded with a hideous screeching blast as sparks and flames shot out in all directions. Kai, Marlowe, and Ryan ran for cover. Max ran out from behind the drum kit to the front of the stage, looking bewildered for a moment at the smoldering amp. He turned to the audience, held his drumsticks high in the air, and shouted, "Thank you, San Francisco, good night!"

Marlowe and Ryan slowly walked toward the center of the stage as the crowd applauded wildly. They looked at each other in confusion and then smiled and waved to the audience before walking offstage.

Kai just stood there for a moment, staring at me with a completely inscrutable expression on his face, before he finally turned and followed the others off the stage.

## Chapter Two: A Violent Reunion

"I am so sorry," I whispered. "Is it completely dead?"

"Yeah, you could say that." Kai stood up, glancing around. "What happened this time?"

"I don't really know. Todd was acting like a jackass again, and I just lost it."

"Todd? What's he doing here?"

"Maggie wanted to see you play, and he tagged along. She has a gigantic crush on you."

"So you assumed I'm sleeping with her," he snapped.

I was taken aback. Kai didn't snap at me. Not ever.

"No, of course not."

Kai took a deep breath. "I'm sorry. I figured this was because of your jealousy again."

"No, Kai, I trust you. I do!" I insisted when he shot me a skeptical look. "It was just that Maggie and Todd were really pissing me off. Ask Michael. He was ready to kill Todd, too."

"That's not saying much. Michael's even more jealous than you are." Kai coiled up a cable, stuffed it into his gear bag, and hefted his guitar over his shoulder. "Listen, I'm not in the best mood right now. Can we talk about this later?"

He picked up his destroyed amp, and I followed him toward the exit, fighting back tears. I'd never seen him so angry. Worse, I'd never seen him act so *cold*. Not with me.

"Kai, hold up!" We turned and saw Marlowe walking toward us with Jeremy, the singer from Hollow Ground.

"Man, that rocked," Jeremy said. "Those were some serious pyrotechnics you pulled off. Totally subversive, just ending the set like that in the middle of a tune. How did you do that?"

Kai glanced at Marlowe, who was looking at him with a mischievous smile, and then at me. "It's kind of a secret," Kai said.

"It hella warmed up the crowd for us. That was the most into it I've ever seen a San Francisco crowd." He lit a cigarette and exhaled deeply. "So check it out: it looks like the band we'd lined up isn't going to be able to tour with us until after the twenty-third, so what do you think about filling in for them until then?"

"Yeah, I think we're available," Kai said. "We'll talk to Max and Ryan."

"Cool. Our manager will call yours. Catch you later, guys." Jeremy strode away, and Marlowe slipped up next to Kai.

"We killed it tonight," she said. "That was crazy when your amp exploded, but hell, we just got more gigs with Hollow!" Her forehead crinkled. "What's wrong?"

"Nothing," he said, glancing at me. "I'm just not quite sure how I'm going to pay for another amp."

"Don't worry, I've got it covered," I said, trying not to sound bitter. Yes, it was really bad that I'd lost control like that. But it was just an amp. It wasn't like anyone got hurt.

"You're a lucky man, Kai," Marlowe said with a smile, just as Michael walked up and wrapped his arms around her.

"Beautiful and smart *and* buys you new gear when you blow yours up." She winked at me, and once again, I felt like a total bitch for ever thinking that she and Kai would cheat on Michael and me.

Kai's expression softened a bit. "I'm beat. We'll see you guys tomorrow, okay?" I followed him out into the night.

"I know a music store in Berkeley that should have what you need," I said. "We can go there in the morning." I was walking quickly, not looking at Kai.

"Thanks."

We got in the car and drove in silence over the Bay Bridge toward my mom's apartment in Berkeley. Finally, I couldn't stand it anymore.

"So again, I'm really sorry. I know I have to work on my self-control. And I hope you know that it had nothing to do with you this time."

"Yeah, I know. But . . . "

"But what?" I asked.

"I think it might be best if maybe you didn't come to my gigs for a while."

I felt like my heart had stopped. "Excuse me?"

"The place was packed. You could have started a fire, could have hurt somebody. And yeah, you weren't directing your anger at me, but you were reacting to Maggie's reaction to me, and to Todd."

"So? I doubt Todd is going to be at any more of your gigs!"

Kai shook his head. "It's just too loaded an issue for you, seeing fans acting that way. Remember the first time you ever shot a fireball?"

"Yes, it was when those assholes nearly killed you, if you'll recall."

"But right before that, you were freaking out about that girl who was hitting on me. Then there's the time you blew up my window because you thought I was cheating on you with Marlowe. And now this. Are you starting to see a pattern?"

I sat fuming in silence. I knew he was right. As much as I'd gotten over my jealousy, as much as I completely trusted him now, there was still that evil part of me that was always lurking, ready to throw a fireball at the person I loved most in the world.

"Ashlyn, remember when you sent me away, for my own safety? Well, now I think you should stay away from my gigs for the safety of everyone else. It's not because I don't want you there, believe me." He took my hand gently in his. "I'm sorry I got so angry. I really liked that amp."

"It sounded great, right up until the explosion."

"If I ever get a sponsorship from a manufacturer, you can blow up all the amps you want. Okay?"

I couldn't help smiling. "Okay. But promise me you'll keep playing for me at home, and that I can come listen to you guys practice sometimes."

He kissed my hand. "Of course." He parked in front of my mom's place and then reached over and pulled me into his arms. "We'll figure this out. You'll find Deimos, and this will all be behind us."

"In theory, anyway." I couldn't help feeling myself sinking into despair. Kai felt I was too dangerous to be at his gigs, and I was no closer to figuring out who Deimos was. How much longer could I live like this?

The next morning, Kai and I didn't say a word about the previous night. We got up late, had breakfast with my mom, and then wandered into the music store almost as if we were just window shopping instead of going intentionally to

21

replace the amp I'd blown up the night before. The shop was packed with equipment. Guitars, amps, drums, keyboards, speakers . . . it was a gearhead's paradise. Kai slowly scrutinized each of the amps, his guitar bag slung over his shoulder.

A middle-age man with shaggy hair approached us. "Can I help you?"

"Looking for a new amp," Kai answered. "I'm considering the Orange TH30."

"Good choice. Gorgeous clean tones, and a beautiful scronchy bite on the distortion channel. Here, try it out."

I watched curiously as Kai took out his guitar, plugged into the amp, and started strumming. His face was a study in intense concentration as he switched between pickups and changed channels on the amp. Notes sang out as his fingers flew along the neck of the guitar, filling the shop with his beautiful playing. The man didn't seem particularly impressed and just stood back and waited patiently while Kai tested another amp.

When he was on his third amp, I started getting antsy. "Kai, I'm going to head down the street to the stationery store, okay? I think they have something I can get mom for her birthday. Just call me when you're ready to buy something."

"I might be here a while. You don't mind?"

"No, of course not. Take your time, make sure you get the right thing." I kissed him and left the shop, his music following me and then stopping abruptly as I closed the door behind me.

As I entered the stationery store, a flood of memories washed over me. I had worked there for three years, right up until I left for UCSB. I didn't miss my crazy boss, Lisa, but it had been fun learning about all the merchandise and meeting the variety of people who came into the store. The smell of lavender wafted through the shop, and classical music played softly in the background.

"Ashlyn, what are you doing here?" I spun around and saw Lisa. I could tell immediately that one of her manic sub-personalities was at the helm that morning.

"Hey, Lisa. Just visiting, and I need a present for my mom."

"What do you think about this?" she asked. "I'm thinking we can move more of these fountain pens if we have a real fountain. But I'm not sure how to work the pens into it."

Tentatively, I walked over to the corner where she was working. In the middle of the floor stood a fountain full of water and gravel. A bunch of pens had been stuck haphazardly in the gravel bed. They looked like dead sticks in a sad, little pond.

Just then, Mark, the assistant manager, walked in carrying the front tire of his bike. "Morning," he said cheerfully as he removed his helmet, then stopped dead when he saw me. "Ashlyn! Holy shit, how are you?" He gave me a big hug and then glanced at the pond project. We rolled our eyes at each other.

"You're late!" Lisa yelled at him.

"Lisa, have you lost weight? You look fantastic," Mark cooed.

She beamed. "I've dropped a pound or two."

"Well, keep up the great work. Before you know it, you'll be doing triathlons like me and Ashlyn." He set his tire and helmet down behind the counter.

Lisa stood back, observing the results of her efforts, then threw her hands in the air. "Make it work, will you? Oh, and you better hurry. I don't want customers to see this mess."

"I wouldn't worry about it," Mark said. "Customers don't start trickling in for another hour."

"I don't recall asking for your opinion," she said archly and stomped into the back room, undoubtedly to call her husband and whine.

I picked up one of the pens. "So nothing's changed, I see."

His face clouded. "It has. She's actually getting weirder. I mean, seriously weird. On Thursday she threw her shoe at the ficus tree."

"Hmm, that is weirder than usual. Any idea why?"

He shrugged. "Ran out of her meds? Who knows?"

A high screech came from the back room, and Mark cringed. A moment later, Lisa came barreling out wearing nothing but an apron, brandishing a feather duster. "This dust is out of hand!" she wailed.

"Oh shit," Mark said under his breath. "Keep her busy for a minute. I'll call Dan." He scurried behind the counter and started whispering into the phone while Lisa marched from plant to plant, dusting them vigorously, her bare bottom jiggling as she worked.

My brain was racing. I had no idea what to say to Lisa to keep her calm while we waited for her husband, so I kept an eye on the front door, ready to deflect any customers who might make an ill-timed stop to buy stationery. A few minutes later, a car pulled up, and Dan rushed in. He looked exhausted. "Lisa, honey, what's going on?"

"Oh, no you don't!" she shouted. "I know exactly what you're after, mister, and you're sick. Sick! There are children present."

Mark and I stared at each other, dumbfounded.

Dan approached her carefully, speaking in a low voice. "Let's get you dressed, honey. Remember that Feng Shui consultant you liked? He's got a friend he wants you to meet.

Doctor Schulz. He's, um, an interior designer. He says he wants to see you right away."

Lisa's eyes turned to angry slits. "Doctor Schulz the interior designer? Do you think I'm stupid?!" She swung at Dan and hit him hard across the face, sending him flying into a display of note cards.

My heart pounded as I raced over to Lisa. Her eyes had become wild, and she screamed and swung at me. I stepped out of the way and grabbed her arms and pinned them behind her. "Mark, go help Dan!" I shouted as Lisa struggled.

"I'm okay," Dan groaned as he got to his feet.

We heard a siren, and then two police officers hurried into the store. Mark ran up to tell them what was going on, and a moment later, they had Lisa handcuffed and were leading her out of the shop, Dan trailing behind with his head hanging low. I felt horrible for both of them.

"You weren't kidding," I said to Mark, who was looking very pale. "She finally lost it."

He shook his head sadly. "It started about a week ago. She's always been kind of nuts, of course, but I never put her down for a certifiable loon. And I never thought she'd turn violent."

"It's all for the best that she finally did so we could have her arrested," I reasoned. "Otherwise, the cops wouldn't have been able to do anything. You can't force people into mental hospitals if they're harmless."

"So now what do I do?" he asked. I noticed his hands were shaking.

"Now you keep her store running. And it's probably a good time to make some of those changes you always wanted to do to bring in more business. She's going to need it."

I walked slowly up the street to the music store. I was haunted by the wild look I'd seen in Lisa's eyes before she tried to hit me. Mental illness made me very squeamish. I would rather watch gory surgeries all day than spend five minutes with crazy people. They were so unsettling, so unpredictable. Like something out of my nightmares.

I entered the shop just as Kai was putting away his guitar. "Perfect timing," he said. "I found just what I wanted, and it's on sale. Plus, Bud is going to put us in touch with his promoter."

"His promoter?"

"Yeah, for his band. Don't look so surprised," he said with a smirk. "Your fingers don't fall off when you hit forty. I heard him play, and he's got great chops."

I glanced over at Bud, the middle-aged guitar salesman, who was ringing up the amp and several packs of strings. I tried to imagine him rocking out on stage and ended up picturing him in nothing but an apron instead. I shuddered.

"Well, we better go. We need to get on the road." I quickly stepped forward and paid for the amp, hurrying us out of the store as fast as I could.

When we got back to Isla Vista that night, we dropped off our things and then went straight to the dojo. I told everyone what had happened at Kai's gig, with Michael filling in the details. John was visibly frustrated.

"I cannot stress enough how important it is that you gain control over this power," he insisted.

"I know, John. I'm trying."

Michael shook his head. "That guy Todd was unbelievable. It took all my self-control not to beat the crap out of him. I almost lost it."

"Yes," John said, "but when you lose control, Michael, you don't risk exposing us by throwing fireballs."

I clenched my fists. "If I could just find Deimos. If I could just find him and defeat him and then we could all get on with our lives."

John cocked his head to the side. "Ashlyn, I'm going to make a recommendation: stop looking. I mean it. You are pushing too hard on this. You need to take a break. Cool off a bit."

"I know the best way to cool off," Christoph chimed in. "Skiing."

"You ski?" I asked him.

"Certainly I ski. I grew up not far from the Alps. We should all go to Bear Mountain this weekend."

I looked around at the others in disbelief. "You seriously think that going skiing is going to solve our problems? Just like that?"

"I think you have to live your life," John said. "Go skiing. Take a break from being a Soterian." I looked at him, aghast. I couldn't believe these words were coming out of his mouth.

I turned to Michael. "Back me up on this, will you?"

He shrugged. "You do seem pretty high-strung. Chilling out on the slopes might help you relax, and that could help you sense Deimos better. Plus, my snowboard hasn't gotten quite enough use in the last couple of years."

"Wonderful!" Christoph said. "I'll make all the arrangements."

Rebecca came and stood next to me. "I think they're right. Let's go pretend we're normal college students for a weekend."

I threw my hands in the air. "Okay, you win. You're all completely nuts, but you win. We'll go up to the slopes and pretend that we don't have a care in the world. Hell, maybe Deimos will be there!"

Christoph laughed. "Maybe I'll sit next to him on the chairlift, and I can push him off."

"Just go and have a good time," John said. "And try to relax."

## Chapter Three: The Last Run

"See? This is so much better!" Christoph said, looking like it was Christmas all over again. He and Michael were standing in front of me in line for the chairlift. Christoph gazed out over the snow. "The conditions are absolutely perfect. It's going to be a great day."

I had to admit that he had a point. Now that I was getting ready to take my first run after not skiing in three years, I was feeling much more anxious about the slopes than about tracking down the ultimate source of evil.

I looked out across the mountain. The blanket of trees was slashed with channels of snow, each dotted with skiers and snowboarders carving wide, serpentine lines. I stamped my skis, trying to keep my toes from freezing as we stood waiting to get on the lift. I had promised myself I would not use my powers, not even to keep myself warm. I had to forget I was a Soterian, and if I fell . . . well, I just hoped like hell that I would simply fall and wouldn't accidentally fly in front of a crowd of people.

Rebecca and I rode up together, huddling together to keep warm. She was just as excited as Christoph was.

"I can't believe there's snow so close to school," she said.

"You call this close? It took like five hours to get here."

"It's still closer than I thought it would be. It must be seventy degrees in I.V. today."

"Don't remind me," I grumbled, rubbing my frozen cheeks with my glove. "I can't believe we're shivering our asses off on a chairlift when we could be on the beach right now."

"As soon as you do a couple runs, you'll change your mind." She lifted the bar, and we prepared to ski off the lift. I edged forward, starting to freak out that I was going to fall, but I was able to glide off the lift and come to a stop by Michael and Christoph with no problem at all.

"Let's go!" Christoph said and charged down the slope. I shook off my fear, bounced a few times to get a feel for my skis, and took off after him.

The wind whistled around my helmet as I picked up speed. I tentatively carved out a few gentle turns, surprised that I still knew how to do this after so many years. I started going faster, cutting more aggressively and taking my turns at sharper angles. Everything was covered in a beautiful blanket of white, and suddenly, memories from my childhood came flooding back. I remembered the first time my sister and I went to the slopes with my dad, who patiently taught us to turn and to stop. Laurel picked it up pretty quickly, while I had a harder time. But once I got it, I fell in love with it, and it wasn't long before I was flying past my sister, who was content to ski in nice, graceful turns while I focused on going as fast as I could without crashing.

I came to a straightaway heading to the bottom of the lift. I got into a tuck and shot straight toward the others, who were all waiting for me to finish my run. Michael's eyes widened as I aimed straight for them, and Christoph leaned protectively in front of Rebecca. At the last second, I jumped into a hockey stop, spraying them all with snow. Michael looked pissed off, and Christoph laughed.

"I'm glad you remember how to stop at least," he said, brushing snow off Rebecca. "Come on, I'll race you down on the next run."

As the day wore on, everything came back to me. Even though I refused to actively use my powers, my excellent new vision made it much easier to see dips and bumps, even in the shaded sections, and my reflexes were amazing, my body responding more quickly than it ever had. I was having the time of my life, and I wasn't getting tired as quickly as I used to. We raced each other down the slopes, and as the sun made its way to the other side of the mountain, casting everything in shadow, we spent some time on the lower slopes doing silly tricks like skiing backwards and on one ski, resulting in some spectacular yard sales. Finally, shivering and covered in snow, we decided to head back in.

"Let's go into the lodge and get some coffee before we hit the road," I suggested. "I'm completely frozen."

"Sounds good to me," Michael agreed. His face was red from the cold, which somehow made him look especially adorable and sexy. I felt heat rising to my face and turned to Christoph and Rebecca.

"Ready to go?" I asked.

"I'm going to take one last run," Christoph said. "Rebecca, you should go in and get warm."

"No, I'll take another run with you," she said. "Let's hurry up, they're closing the lift in a few minutes."

Michael and I made our way to the lodge while Christoph and Rebecca caught the lift to the summit. "I have to admit," I said to him, "that you guys were right. I've barely thought about The Evil One at all today."

"That's an interesting nickname for Kai."

31

"Very funny. You know what I mean. Besides, I can only imagine the nicknames you have for Marlowe. Pookie? Or maybe Lolo?"

Michael's face turned scarlet. "Shut up," he muttered.

"Wait, is that really it? You call her Lolo?" I laughed. "Well, I guess that's better than Pookie. It's kind of cute, actually."

We clomped along in our heavy ski boots to the coffee bar and then sat down with large, steaming mochas. I inhaled the rich aroma and sipped slowly, sighing at the magnificent feeling of the coffee warming my throat and stomach. Michael looked deep in thought.

"What's up?" I asked.

He looked up at me, then down at his coffee again. "Just thinking about, you know, stuff."

"Oh, stuff. Of course. Thanks for clearing that up."

"No, it's just . . . it's all just weird. The way I feel about Marlowe. I've never felt like this about anyone. Close," he said, looking into my eyes in a way that made my heart stop, "but not like this. You know what I mean?"

"I know exactly what you mean," I said softly.

"Yeah. I guess you do. You knew right away with Kai, didn't you?"

"From the first moment I saw him. And based on what your heart sounded like when you first saw Marlowe, I'd say it was the same thing for you. Even though you'd had your eye on a truly fantastically amazing woman before you met her," I said, smirking at him, "there was no comparison. She's your soulmate. Of course it's never felt like this before."

His eyes searched mine. "I don't believe in soulmates and fate and all that crap."

I shrugged. "Call it whatever you want. Your heart knows the truth."

Just then, I gasped as I felt a horrible stabbing pain in my chest. A wave of panic and grief washed over me, and I grabbed the edge of the table.

"What's wrong?" Michael asked in alarm.

I reached out with my feelings, and I could practically hear Rebecca screaming. The pain coming from her was so intense it felt like it would bring down the entire mountain. But it wasn't physical pain.

Michael read my expression, and we both jumped to our feet and sprinted for the door. Michael ducked behind a clump of trees. I caught up with him a few seconds later, amazed at how fast he could run in ski boots. I turned my back to him, and as he wrapped his arm around my chest, we disappeared and rose into the sky.

"Who is it?" he asked.

"All I can feel is Rebecca in agony. I can't feel anything from Christoph at all."

"Shit," he swore under his breath. I picked up speed, heading straight up the mountain. It was easy to tell where Rebecca was . . . her ragged emotions were like a beacon. A few minutes later, I spotted her blue jacket and black hair against the snow.

"Rebecca!" I shouted and zoomed toward her. She was lying face down, her body convulsing.

"Christoph!" she screamed. I noticed that she was at the edge of a crevasse, her head hanging down into the opening. Michael and I landed next to her and reappeared.

"What is it? What happened?" I demanded.

"It's Christoph!" she wailed. "One moment he was skiing just ahead of me, and the next moment he disappeared! I can't see anything. Ashlyn, you have to go after him!"

I looked around to see whether anyone was watching us, but we were alone on the slope. I hovered over the hole and then slowly lowered myself down. It was a narrow crevasse, not more than two feet wide, and the light immediately changed from a pale blue to a deep purple. I would soon be in total darkness.

"Christoph!" I shouted. "Can you hear me?" There was no reply. I started to drift farther down when suddenly I heard a whooshing sound. A moment later, snow began heaping down on top of me.

"It's caving in! Get back from the edge!" I shouted, my mouth filling with snow. I tried swimming upward, but the heavy snow was pushing me down. In desperation, I gathered fire in my core and shot a burst of flame over my head. The snow instantly melted and showered me with icy water. I gasped and shot up to the surface, where Rebecca was sitting looking stunned.

I fell onto the snow and gasped for air. I was soaked through and shivering, and I had to keep generating fire in my core to keep myself from freezing.

"I'm sorry," I said breathlessly. "It collapsed." I looked over and saw that the hole was now nothing more than a large wide depression on the slope. At that moment, a man in a ski patrol jacket skied up to us and skidded to a stop.

"Is everything okay?" he asked.

"There's been a cave in, and our friend is down there," Michael answered. "But the opening collapsed. It nearly took her, too." I thought he sounded awfully calm considering his best friend had just disappeared.

And that's when it hit me. Christoph had disappeared. We would never see him again.

As the ski patroller called on his radio for help, I heard a roaring in my ears. I leaned over and threw up.

I crawled over to Rebecca and put my arms around her. She was crying quietly, and the look on her face was such a vivid expression of torture and despair, I would have nightmares about it for years to come. I rocked her gently as she cried. Michael sat silently by, and I could feel his helplessness permeate the air around him like a toxic gas.

"They'll find him," I said softly as Rebecca wept. "He was probably just knocked out or something. I've read tons of stories about people who lived under avalanches for days before they were finally rescued."

"I can't feel him, I can't feel him," Rebecca chanted, rocking back and forth in my arms. "He's gone."

## Chapter Four: The Search

At seven o'clock, we sat in the restaurant in silence, staring at our untouched dinners. The ski patrol had combed the slope, but they couldn't find the opening again. There was no way to reach Christoph, wherever he was. It had been a very deep crevasse and probably dumped into a cavern in the ground. Which meant he could be miles underground for all we knew.

Rebecca and I were both reaching out with our feelings as far as we could, but we couldn't pick up a thing. I had waited by the crevasse as the ski patrol worked, straining to listen as hard as possible for Christoph, but there was only the sound of the shovels in the snow.

Finally, at the insistence of the ski patrol, we had accepted a ride on a snowmobile and returned to the lodge to warm up. I was nearly frozen from my dousing in the melted snow, and my Alchemist powers had faded. Once again, right when I needed them, they were gone.

Gone. Christoph was gone. I looked at Michael and Rebecca, but their expressions were blank. There was simply no way to fathom life without Christoph. How could he be gone? It was as impossible as the sun disappearing from the sky.

I had no idea what to do next. I couldn't think of a single way to make things better. I considered flying up there after dark and trying to melt the snow, but I'd pretty much have to melt the whole mountain to open that hole again.

"We'd better get a hotel for the night," Rebecca said dully.

"Good thinking," I said. I pulled out my phone and looked up nearby hotels. Rebecca sat staring out the window. I couldn't read her expression or her feelings, other than a hollow ache.

"Not to sound like an asshole, but shouldn't we go home?" Michael asked.

I gaped at him. "Are you serious?"

"I just don't see what we can do here. If we go home, we can at least look in his stuff for his parent's information. We need to call them and let them know."

"Let them know what?" Rebecca asked. Her eyes had a cold, hard look in them that I'd never seen before. It made my heart skip a beat. "You can go where you want, but I'm not leaving until we've found him."

Michael bit his lip. "They've called off the search. What do you propose we do?"

"We're Soterians," she shot back. "We'll think of something."

I called a hotel while Rebecca returned to staring out the window and Michael looked deep in thought. I wasn't sure how much Rebecca could feel just then, but I felt intense pain coming from Michael. Christoph was his best friend. *Is* his best friend, I reminded myself. Even though there was very little chance that he was still alive, Christoph was a Sentry. That kind of strength had to offer him some protection, even against a mountain of snow.

Early the next morning, the ski patrol resumed its search. Rebecca and I stood at the window in the lodge, watching them in the distance. In their red jackets, they looked like tiny spots of blood against the white snow. I tried not to let my mind go in that direction. I had been up half the night, waking from nightmares of falling through the snow and landing right in front of Christoph, whose lifeless face was blue and frostbitten. I shuddered from the memory and glanced at Rebecca. The dark circles under her eyes suggested that she'd slept even less than I had.

We waited in the lodge all day. They had closed the run where Christoph had fallen through and had brought large machines to try to dig out the hole, but as time wore on, our hope faded more and more.

Finally, as the sun went over the other side of the mountain, we saw the red dots slowly move down the hill. Rebecca stiffened, and we pulled on our jackets and headed outside to meet them.

The ski patrol guy who had found us the previous day was the first to arrive at the lodge. He approached us wearily.

"We've done everything we can," he said. "It's no use. Every time we try to dig it out, it fills with snow again."

"So what do we do now?" I asked.

"That's what I'm trying to say. There's nothing else to be done."

I paused as his words sank in. "You mean you're just giving up? We're just going to leave him down there to die?"

"I'm afraid the chances of finding him alive are pretty slim now. There's another storm heading in tonight, and temperatures are going to drop well below freezing. We have to call off the search. I'm very sorry." He looked at both of us with sad eyes and walked away.

I turned to Rebecca. "This is insane. They can't just give up like that."

"They made the right decision. They can't risk hurting anyone else." She turned to me. "Go back to Santa Barbara, Ashlyn. Go and find his parents' phone number and let them know what happened."

"What are you going to do?" I asked.

"I'm not leaving. Not without Christoph. Even if that means I have to wait until the snow melts in the spring, I'm not leaving here."

"Rebecca . . ."

"No," she said firmly. "The last twenty four hours have been the hardest in my life, and it's made some things completely clear to me." She looked down, and I noticed she was shaking. "I cannot go back to Santa Barbara until I've seen his face again. Dead or alive."

I put my arm around her. "Bec, I'm not ready to leave yet, either. I'm going to scout around, see if I can pick up anything. If I can't find anything, I'll leave tomorrow. But I need another night."

Michael took a step toward us. "Come on, Rebecca, I'll take you back to the hotel." I looked into his face and noticed that he had circles under his eyes, too. This had to be almost as hard on him as it was for Rebecca. As they walked back into the lodge, I ducked under the deck, disappeared, and flew up the slope.

That night, I walked into the hotel room shivering with cold. I'd spent four hours flying around, trying to melt the snow again, and calling out to Christoph, but there was nothing. Just a silent void. When the snow started falling so hard that I couldn't see anymore, I gave up and headed back to the hotel.

Rebecca looked up expectantly when I walked in, but her face fell the second she read my feelings. She walked slowly over to me and put her hands on my arms, filling me with healing that brought the feeling back into my fingers and toes.

"Thanks, Bec. I'm so sorry. I didn't find a trace of him. How are you doing?"

Her face clouded. "How do you think I'm doing?"

"Sorry, stupid question."

She shook her head. "That's not what I mean. I mean can't you feel what I'm feeling?"

I reached out with my senses, but I felt nothing. "No, not at all."

She sighed and sat down heavily on the bed. "You stayed out there too long. You're half-frozen and you can't pick up on what I'm feeling, even though I'm a train wreck. Your Alchemist powers are gone again."

"I know. But I thought I could at least see or hear something."

She crawled under the covers. "Let's get some sleep. We'll try again in the morning."

"But Rebecca, can he survive another night?"

She looked hard at me. "This is Christoph we're talking about. He's a Sentry. If anyone can survive, it's him. And if he can't, I still need to find him."

I got into bed and turned out the light. When I closed my eyes, all I saw were snowflakes, and when I finally drifted off to sleep, I dreamed of Christoph again, deep below the snow.

At three o'clock in the morning, I jolted awake. Rebecca was sitting upright, her eyes wide in the dark.

"What is it?" I asked.

"I was having a nightmare," she said. "Christoph was trying to reach me, but I was too far away." She threw back the covers. "Ashlyn, I think he's alive."

She got up and hurriedly pulled on her clothes. I followed her lead. Secretly, I knew we were on another fool's errand, but I didn't say a word. I had some experience with grieving, and I knew how important it was to feel like you've tried everything before you give up.

We bundled up and trudged out into the bitter cold. I looked to make sure nobody was around, then disappeared as Rebecca put her arms around my neck. She jumped up on my back, and we flew into the darkness. The snow had stopped, but there was still a thick blanket of clouds hanging low in the sky, blocking out the moonlight. I headed for the ski resort, which was a disorienting three blocks in the freezing, dark night. But I found that I was able to generate some heat in my core, and Rebecca, who was already shivering, clung tighter to me.

We found the ski resort and flew toward the slope where Christoph had disappeared. Rebecca was silent, and I could feel her straining with all her might to try to sense Christoph. Once again, there was nothing. I sighed, trying not to give in to my frustration. I knew there was no point in trying to find him now. We might as well wait until the snow melted, and then we could excavate and try to find his body—

"Shhh!" Rebecca warned. I hadn't said anything out loud, but she was reaching out so hard with her feelings that my own must have seemed like shouts to her. Suddenly, she stiffened.

"What is it?" I asked.

"That way!" she shouted. "Quick!"

I flew us across the mountain and around a bend. I paused for a moment, about to ask her where to go, but that's when I felt it.

Christoph.

It was unmistakable. I felt his pain, determination, and half-crazed panic. I dropped to the ground, and Rebecca fell to her feet.

"Help me!" she yelled as she started digging in a snow bank near the bottom of a slope.

"Step back," I said. I summoned all the fire I could in my core and then sent a slow stream of flame toward the snow. It hissed and steamed as a large hole began to open up. Suddenly, I saw movement, and I pulled back the fire, gathering it into a fireball and letting it hover near the hole, where it cast an orange glow into the opening.

A fist punched through the snow. Then another fist appeared. And then Christoph's entire body burst through, falling face forward onto the ground.

Rebecca shrieked and threw herself onto him. She rolled him over, and I gasped when I saw that his pale, blue face looked just as it had in my dreams. His lips were white and chapped and looked like they were made of ice. His hands, purple and swollen, were clenched into fists. But his breath puffed into the air like steam from a train engine.

I ran over and put my hands on Christoph's chest. Rebecca and I poured healing into him with everything we had. The fireball quickly faded and was finally extinguished, plunging us into darkness again. Spots swam before my eyes as I felt the life draining out of me. The only sound was all three of us breathing hard, our hearts pounding.

"Rebecca?" Christoph suddenly asked in a weak voice.

"Yes, Christoph, I'm here. You're going to be okay. Ashlyn and I are healing you. Just lie back and you'll be fine in no time." Her voice was thick with tears.

But he didn't lie still. I felt him suddenly sit up, and I created a small fireball to shed some light. He grabbed Rebecca's face in his hands and looked into her eyes with such an intense, overwhelming look of longing and joy and pain and love all at once that my eyes filled with tears. Rebecca was crying hard now, and he kissed her gently on her trembling lips. She threw her arms around him and they held each other, rocking back and forth, all three of us sobbing as we sat in the snow, unable to believe what had just happened.

That moment was burned into my memory forever. Even if I live to be a hundred years old, I will never, ever forget that night and the look on Christoph's face when he first saw Rebecca after spending thirty-five hours digging himself out of the snow.

## Chapter Five: Silence and Other Noises

Christoph spent a couple of nights in the hospital, telling and retelling his story to astonished ski patrollers and doctors who came by to visit him. Everyone was amazed that he had survived, let alone dug himself out, and nobody could figure out why he didn't have frostbite. I was annoyed with Rebecca for healing him so completely that first night instead of letting him finish the final stages on his own. After all, wasn't she the one who had lectured me about the very same thing when I'd fractured my arm? But I could hardly blame her. Christoph was making a fast recovery, whereas something was definitely different about Rebecca.

When we arrived home two days later, Ryan and Toby welcomed us, and Christoph had to tell his story all over again.

"Dude, you must have been freaked out," Ryan said. "How did you deal with being under all that snow?"

"I just kept going," he explained. "I had a good reason to come home." He took Rebecca's hand and smiled at her, but she didn't smile back.

"The lack of food alone would have killed Ryan," Toby said. "And on that subject, you're probably ready for something better than hospital food, so we set you up." Toby went into the kitchen and came back with two steaming pizzas he'd just pulled from the oven. "Sausage, pepperoni, ham, chicken, and salami. Figured that would get your strength back."

Christoph's eyes bulged. He grabbed two slices, folded them over like a sandwich, and shoved them happily into his mouth. "Fank oo," he said through a mouthful of food. He took a slice and put it on a plate for Rebecca. She smiled at him, but she only picked at her food, barely eating for the rest of the evening.

"Hey Toby, aren't you going to show everyone the photo?" Ryan asked between bites.

Toby slapped his forehead. "I can't believe I almost forgot!" He jumped to his feet and dashed out of the room, and Rebecca and I only had a moment to exchange quizzical glances before he returned carrying a large folder. "It's the cover for *Silence and Other Noises*. Our album," he explained. "Take a look!"

We crowded around as he opened the folder. Inside was a black and white photo of the band on the bluffs at sunset. Max was sitting on the ground, staring off into the distance. Ryan was leaping into the air. Kai was standing in the foreground, his arms wrapped around the body of his guitar with the neck pointed downward, his chin resting on the guitar. Marlowe was in the front, her body turned toward Kai as she looked over her shoulder at the camera, her hair gently blowing in the wind. Little details were colored in, including her lips, the pick guard on Kai's guitar, Ryan's shoes, and the tattoo on Max's arm.

Everyone immediately started talking about how gorgeous the photo was, how it evoked a sense of mystery and coolness. But Michael and I were silent, unable to stop staring at the image. Kai and Marlowe looked so stunning,

45

each so beautiful and photogenic, their beauty magnified off each other. Marlowe's irresistible combination of sultry and vulnerable, and Kai's soulful expression that made it feel like he was looking right through you, were addictive.

I felt Kai's warm arms wrap around me. "What do you think?" he asked.

I tore my gaze away from the photo and kissed him softly. "It's perfect. You've got both the look and the sound now. Better hire some bodyguards, because you guys are going to have to fight off the fans with a stick."

Michael quietly left the room. As I watched him go, I felt his worry and tension mingle with my own. That photo was going to cause a lot of people to fall in love with Marlowe and Kai, and although I felt sure Marlowe had plenty of experience dealing with men coming on to her, I wasn't sure how Kai was going to handle it. I glanced over at Rebecca, wondering if she was picking up on my concern, but she was sitting next to Christoph looking absorbed by her private thoughts, clearly not listening to what he was saying.

When we left The Manor and walked back to our apartment later that evening, Rebecca continued her distracted silence. She didn't say anything as she changed into her pajamas and barely answered me when I asked her a question about school. Finally, as she got into bed, I sat down next to her. "Do you want to talk about it?" I asked.

"I guess I should . . . " her voice trailed away.

"Take your time, Bec. This has been a big shock. I'm here for you when you want to talk, okay?"

She looked down. "He asked me to marry him."

My heart stopped. "Excuse me?"

"At the hospital yesterday, when you left to get coffee." She pushed back the covers and moved to the window, gazing out into the courtyard. "He said that falling in the crevasse was the best thing that ever happened to him, that it gave him the time to think about everything and get clarity on what he wanted out of life. And that the most important thing in life was me."

Her words sank in. "Are you serious? You are serious. My God, what did you say?"

She turned and looked at me. "I said yes."

I got up hesitantly. "So . . . so this is a really good thing! So then why aren't we celebrating?"

She twisted a lock of hair around her finger. "It feels wrong, somehow. To be celebrating when we just went through such hell. When I think of all those people who searched for him for days, and all the pain . . . "

I put my arms around her. "My Alchemist powers were gone, so I can only imagine what it must have been like to have to feel everyone else's pain on top of your own. It's no wonder you're still reeling from it. Christoph had a lot of time to sort through his feelings, and now you need time to decompress, too. You're like a sponge that's all full of water and can't take in one more drop."

At that, she started sobbing, and I held her as she cried out all the anguish, pain, and anxiety she'd been holding for days. When her tears finally subsided, I helped her into bed and went to get her a glass of water. When I returned, she was already fast asleep.

I stared at her as she slept. She looked so young. Way too young to be getting married, and with our missions as Soterians . . .

I lay back on my bed. I just had to find Deimos so we could get on with our lives. If anything, our trip to the snow, ironically intended to help me relax, had only reaffirmed my conviction that nothing mattered as much as finding Deimos. Who was he, anyway? And once I did find him, how in the hell was I going to defeat him if he couldn't be destroyed? He had supernatural powers, sure, but he had to have taken on a human form. What would happen if we "killed" the body he was in? I wished I could find someone who had gone up against him before, but the Soterians were so secret that most units didn't even know about each other. According to John, the fact that our unit had joined up with the San Francisco unit was remarkably rare. My mind churned as I went over my history with the Soterians so far, trying to piece together some kind of threads that would lead me to Deimos.

Where was I?

Oh no, not this dream again.

I was floating down a dark, narrow hallway of moss-covered stone. The only sound I could hear above my thumping heartbeat was the slow drip of water that seeped between the rocks and coated the floor in a slick pool. Even as I approached the candlelit chamber at the end of the hall, I knew what was waiting there for me. I stiffened as I saw the figure dressed all in black, his back turned to me. I felt bile rise in my throat. I hated him with every fiber of my being. What would it be this time? Would he torture Kai? Rape Rebecca? Murder Christoph? Whatever fresh evil he devised to haunt my dreams, I was always powerless. My limbs never worked, my scream would get caught in my throat, and my powers were always gone.

A memory floated past, almost like a breeze. Of something my mom had told me about once. Lucid dreaming, I think she called it, where you could take control of your dreams. There were several books on it at the metaphysical bookstore where she worked, and I remembered her telling me it had something to do with first recognizing that you're dreaming, which allows you to take hold of the situation and change it. Well, I'd recognized this as a dream plenty of times, and that never seemed to stop Deimos from carrying out his sadistic acts. But as he turned toward me, another idea hit me. Maybe I couldn't stop Deimos, but what if it weren't Deimos at all?

The candlelight flooded his face. It was Michael. It worked! I had cast Deimos out of my dream! Then I noticed that Michael was staring at me with the same intensity he used to, that look that made me feel like I was about to be devoured, body and soul. Shit, this wasn't really what I had in mind. But once again, I was completely powerless. He walked slowly toward me, and no matter how hard I tried, I couldn't move or speak. I couldn't even turn away as his gaze held mine, his eyes blazing, his breathing fast and shallow. He grabbed my head in both hands and kissed me, hard. The heat emanating from his body was like fire, and I felt my muscles weaken until my legs gave way completely.

He slipped one hand down behind my back, and in one smooth motion he lay me down on the hard, stone floor. Without a word, he tore off his shirt to expose what had to be the most beautiful and perfect body in the universe, and I felt a rush of excitement even as I lay there completely helpless, pleading silently for this not to happen, and at the same time wanting it so desperately. He lay on top of me, and suddenly I could move again. But instead of kicking him off of me, my body responded as if it belonged to someone else, kissing him just as hard as he was kissing me, digging my fingers into the solid muscles of his back, fire coursing through my veins. The longing was unbearable, and my heart pounded wildly as I felt him reach down between us . . .

My eyes popped open. Rebecca was snoring softly, and an owl hooted in the night. I tore back my covers and stomped into the bathroom, where I splashed cold water on my face, trying to bring myself back to reality as waves of sickening guilt and anger washed over me. *It was only a dream*, I kept telling myself, but the attraction between Michael and me was real. How could I have spent so much time and energy worrying that Kai was going to cheat on me when I was the one who had this insane infatuation with Michael? I knew I'd never act on it in real life, but now I had yet another dream to keep me from sleeping well at night. Just how many demons could I carry around in my head, anyway?

I could almost hear Deimos' cold laughter echoing in the back of my mind.

## Chapter Six: Outbreak

"Ashlyn? What's gotten into you?" I heard Michael say. He and I were partnered up in training the next day, and I found it almost impossible to look at him. Kai couldn't make it to training because he had to work an extra shift, so instead of rotating around, I ended up partnered with Michael for the whole session. I kept blushing and stumbling and acting like an idiot. I was so embarrassed and angry at myself, which of course only made things worse.

Rebecca cast sideways glances at me a couple of times as she trained with Christoph, but being the true friend that she was, she didn't say a word about what she was undoubtedly picking up from me. Hell, with the pheromones I was probably giving off, I was surprised that they couldn't all feel it. I took a deep breath and tried to focus.

"Just not feeling too great. Stressful week and all that," I explained.

He eyed me curiously but didn't say anything else.

"Time for work on pressure points," John called out. Oh, great. Michael reached out and grabbed my wrist, and I felt an electric spark shoot between us. I quickly pressed a pressure point on his arm and broke free.

"Nice," he said. "That felt really natural. Now you grab me."

I reached out and took his wrist, feeling the muscles in his forearm tense under my grip. "No, let's do a choke hold instead," he suggested. He turned his back to me, and I hesitated. "Go on, grab me around the neck."

I stepped up to him and reached around his neck. The scent of his sweat distracted me, and I was caught by surprise when he reached up behind him, grabbed the back of my neck, and flipped me over his shoulder as he bent over. I flew through the air and came to a stop an inch above the practice mat we had laid on the floor.

"Time out," John said wearily. Michael reached out his hand to help me up, but I just drifted back into a standing position. My cheeks were hot and probably beet red.

"I think she's sick or something," Michael said to John as he approached us.

"Michael, would you excuse us for a moment? Ashlyn, please follow me." I tried not to hang my head and look like a schoolgirl being punished as I followed John to the back of the dojo. I could feel everyone's eyes on me, which only made my cheeks flush more. When John turned to face me, I tried to keep my face neutral, but I knew I never succeeded in looking innocent.

"So," he began. "You seem to be having some trouble concentrating today. And it seems to be more than just the after-effects of nearly losing Christoph." The expression in his ice-blue eyes told me that he knew exactly what was going on.

"I don't know what's wrong with me," I said weakly. "This is the worst it's ever been, and I don't know why."

"Aside from the fact that you're a healthy twenty-one year-old? Cut yourself some slack, Ashlyn. This time of your life tends to be dominated by your hormones."

"Does it get easier as you get older?" I asked hopefully.

He smiled. "Somewhat. You have to learn to work around it. And my guess is that it's especially bad right now because you're repressing feelings you need to deal with. How are you and Kai doing?'

"Fine," I answered automatically. "Well, actually, not completely fine. He doesn't want me to come to his gigs until I can get my anger problem under control. Fireballs and all that. I know he's right, but it still sucks."

John looked serious. "I know Kai is very busy with work and school and training, and now with his band doing so well, but you have to find time to spend together, alone. Make sure you're channeling your energy appropriately with him so it doesn't come out in other ways." He glanced over at Michael, who was practicing kicks with inhuman speed and ridiculously flawless technique. "You've overcome a major hurdle by learning to trust Kai, but as I've said before, relationships are a constant balancing act. If you let them go off course, it takes great effort to bring them back to center."

He dismissed us for the day, and the four of us got into Rebecca's car and headed back to the apartment. I was silent as Christoph chatted happily about his plans to visit New York with Rebecca over spring break, which was a couple of weeks away. He was planning to ask Rebecca's parents for permission to marry her, which was really freaking her out. I had suggested that maybe they wait and have an "unofficial" engagement for a while, like Kai and I were doing. But Christoph always just shook his head at the suggestion.

"What I learned from being trapped in the snow is that there's no point in waiting for the things you want," he explained. "It can all be taken away from you so quickly." It was hard to argue with that logic, but as I watched Rebecca's nervous face as Christoph talked about how excited he was, I wondered whether his new approach to life came at a heavy price.

As we crossed the complex toward our apartment, we ran into Morgan, the manager. She always treated us with an awed caution since we had busted her last fall for selling drugs to students and then helped save her life. Personally, I was surprised that she still wanted to manage the complex, but she said she wanted her life to be as normal as possible. She greeted us as we approached.

"Rebecca, Ashlyn, I've been wanting to talk to you. I have some news about Tracy."

"What is it?" we both asked. Our roommate, Tracy, had been in rehab for the last few months, and we'd been wondering when she'd be back.

"Her treatment program is coming to an end, and she's decided to leave UCSB and move back home. All in all, I think it's the right choice for her." Rebecca and I nodded in agreement, and I could feel the relief coming from Rebecca. We never liked Tracy, and we both wondered whether we could have done more for her if we'd been better friends to her. "So I have a new roommate assigned to take her place. Her name is Lili, and she'll be moving in at the end of spring break."

"What's she like?" Rebecca asked.

"She seems nice. She's a Theater major with a minor in Math. Tracy's parents are going to come help get her packed up next weekend, so I just wanted to give you a heads up." She looked awkwardly at me. Thanks to Kelly, Kai's ex-girlfriend and possibly the most irritating person in the world, Tracy's parents thought I was the one who had gotten

Tracy hooked on drugs. I hoped Tracy had set the record straight by now, but I wasn't exactly anxious to see them again. In fact, I really wanted to put Tracy and that whole chapter of my life behind me completely.

"Theater major with a minor in Math," Rebecca mused as we climbed the stairs to our apartment. "Seems like an odd combination."

"Ten bucks says that the major is for her and the minor is for her parents," I said. "Either that or she just really likes to play it safe and hedge her bets."

"I just hope she's a little bit neater than Tracy was."

"That's not setting the bar too high."

Rebecca looked sideways at me as she unlocked the front door of our apartment. "So, um, do you want to talk about what's going on?"

"You mean why I was blushing and acting like a total moron during training? Probably about as much as you want to talk about Christoph asking your parents for your hand in marriage."

Rebecca looked down and started anxiously twirling a strand of hair around her finger. "I've never seen him so determined. It's kind of like he thinks it's going to erase what happened to him."

"Well, even Christoph had to be kind of messed up from that experience," I said gently. "Be patient with him. And try to encourage him to at least delay the wedding for a few years. If you tell him you're not ready, he'll understand."

She nodded. "So what are you going to do about the whole Michael thing?"

"There's nothing I can do except spend more time with Kai. It'll pass eventually."

She bit her lip. "Do you think it has something to do with your frustration over our lack of progress on finding Deimos?

I mean, Deimos and Michael are both out of reach for you, so maybe your frustration about one spills over into your frustration about the other."

"Hmm," I mused. "Sounds just like the kind of sick, twisted scenario I would get myself into. And yeah, if we found Deimos and kicked his ass tomorrow, I suspect this whole thing with Michael would fade pretty fast. Until then, I'm stuck." I flopped down on the sofa. "Anyway, to hell with all that. Let's talk about spring break. What are you going to do in New York?"

Just then, my phone rang. "Hey, Kai, I thought you were at work."

"I am, but I got a call from Paul." Paul was a Keeper, like Kai, but for the San Francisco unit. My heart raced a little as I pressed the speaker button on my phone.

"I've put you on speaker so Rebecca can hear. Go ahead. What's going on?"

His voice was thick with concern. "Kenji had to fly home to Seattle. His parents are really sick, and they don't know what's wrong with them."

"Are they in the hospital?" Rebecca asked.

"Worse. They're in a mental ward. They've had some kind of breakdown."

She frowned. "Both at the same time?"

"Apparently so. Theresa got a strong sense that this has something to do with Deimos, so she wants us to have a meeting tonight."

I felt the room sway. Of all my nightmares about Deimos, the ones where he came after my family were by far the worst.

That night, we gathered at John's house and started the call. Kenji, who was the San Francisco unit's Sentry and also a computer geek, had insisted that we start using video conferencing instead of just phone calls, so we squeezed together around John's computer, where we could see Kenji in one window and the rest of the San Francisco unit in another. Theresa, their Mentor, was sitting closest to the camera and was wearing her usual serious expression. Next to her was Jesse, their Scout, who was dressed in a fabulous outfit probably of his own making. He struck a sharp contrast to Raina, their Warrior, whose messy blonde hair and skater clothes concealed her lethal nature. On the other side of Raina was Claire, their Empath, who looked deeply concerned. She was studying Psychology at UC Berkeley, so I was interested to hear what she had to say about this.

Theresa started right in. "Here's what we know. There have been several cases of unexplained, sudden-onset mental illness across the United States. Claire hasn't seen any in the clinic where she's interning, but Kenji has run the numbers, and it looks like it could become much more widespread. Kenji, do you want to comment?"

"Yes," he said. I noticed that he looked pretty worked. "I put together a model, and the projection shows that over the last forty-five days, there's been an increase of over five hundred percent in unexplained mental illness. When you factor out things like age, you see that it's ten times that in the general population where this type of mental illness is rarely seen."

"Is there any geographic pattern, or is it all over the map?" Kai asked.

"All over. There appear to be some clusters of cases, but nothing definitive that ties them together yet."

"Theresa, why do you think Deimos is behind this?" Rebecca asked.

"Because it's exactly the type of thing that causes widespread panic and can have a devastating impact on the economy. Rumors will start circulating about what's causing it, and consumers will stop buying those products until they're proven safe. But once a rumor starts, it's very hard to stop it and to regain the confidence of buyers. That kind of fear and economic hardship on a large scale means an instant increase in Deimos' strength."

"So what's our next step?" Michael asked.

"We need to find out what's causing it before we can find a cure," Claire said. "I've talked to one of the psychiatrists at the clinic, and he said that it can take a long time to develop treatments for these kinds of problems."

"But with computer modeling," Kenji argued, "we can find a cure in a much shorter amount of time. A high school student found a potential cure for Cystic Fibrosis this way. Researchers are infuriatingly slow to adopt new methods, so while they're getting around to entering the twenty-first century, I'm going ahead with my own program." He took a sip of coffee, and I wondered how long he'd been working on this.

"Kenji, how are your parents doing?" Rebecca asked.

He looked down. "Not good. They don't know who I am." There was a pause as this sank in for all of us.

"Kenji has taken a leave of absence from his classes at Berkeley," Theresa explained. "His professors have allowed him to do this project for credit, and he's also teaming up with students at the University of Washington."

"What can we do to help?" Christoph asked.

Theresa shook her head. "Nothing right now, but be on alert. Once we have more information, we'll need to start checking out possible connections."

We talked more about the details of the disease and ended the call with promises to do everything we could to help Kenji, but I had a really bad feeling about this particular mission. Unlike the drug epidemic we fought, this wasn't just targeting young, otherwise healthy students. This was targeting everyone, young and old, healthy and sick. And it was only a matter of time before it killed someone.

## Chapter Seven: Lili

"Not bad. A few touches here and there, some decent artwork, and it'll feel like home."

Rebecca and I stood back and watched as Lili circled the living room, her hands resting casually on her slim hips. She sat on the sofa and bounced a few times, her short black hair flopping into her face, and then headed for Tracy's room. "This the room?"

"Um, yeah, but Tracy hasn't moved out yet," I replied, casting a glance at Rebecca.

"That's cool, I'll just take a peek . . . whoa, she's kind of a slob." Lili wrinkled her aquiline nose and shut the door, then gazed around, looking satisfied. "Yeah, this will be just fine."

Rebecca and I both stared at Lili, completely unsure of what to make of her. She had shown up out of the blue, announced that she was Lili Zamani, our new roommate, and that she had stopped by to have a look at the apartment.

"When are you moving in exactly?" Rebecca asked.

"End of spring break," she answered, picking a piece of string off her shirt and flicking it onto the carpet. "I've got six performances that week and can't even think about moving before then. Just needed to check out the space and see what needs to be done before I move in."

"And, um, what do you think?" I asked tentatively, not at all liking where this might be going.

She peered at me. "Needs a few things here and there. Don't worry, I'm not going to come in here and take over your space. We'll be all democratic about it, of course, but I really don't think you're going to mind what I'm bringing."

"Morgan said you're a theater major and minoring in Math?" Rebecca asked.

"Double major, actually. Weird combo, I know, but I insisted on studying what I wanted."

"And your parents insisted that you study Math?" I asked, looking smugly at Rebecca.

Lili cocked her head. "No, I wanted to study *both* theater and Math. Hence the double major." She spoke patiently as if she were speaking to a small child, and I felt like an ass.

"Where do your parents live?" Rebecca asked. Lili traipsed into the kitchen, opened a few cupboards, stuck her nose in one of them, and then shut them again.

"They're still in Iran. They're furious that I'm not coming back for spring break, but that's the breaks. So to speak. They'd be even more furious if they knew why."

I moved closer to the kitchen, where Lili was now looking in the freezer. "What play are you in?"

She strolled back into the living room and approached the window, pulling back the curtain to look out into the courtyard. "It's more of a performance art piece than a play. Explores the syncretic relationship between irony and truth through the vehicle of performative auto-eroticism."

There was a long pause before Rebecca finally spoke. "I'm sorry, did you, are you going to . . . did you say you're going to masturbate on stage?"

"I don't think of it as masturbation," Lili said, closing the curtain again, "so much as animating a scathing indictment of the lies we tell ourselves every day. Anyway, thanks for letting me pop in early. It was nice to meet you."

With that, she walked out of the living room and closed the front door behind her. I looked at Rebecca, who was twirling her hair around her finger.

"I'm not sure what to think," she said in answer to my silent question.

"Well, she's a step up from Tracy, anyway. And who knows? We might get something good out of this situation."

"How so?"

"Maybe she'll give us free passes to her shows."

Rebecca gaped at me and burst out laughing. Then I started laughing, and pretty soon, we had collapsed on the sofa and were laughing so hard there were tears streaming down our faces.

"See?" I said when I could finally speak again. "She's already made things better. That's the first good laugh we've had since . . . a long time."

Rebecca wiped her eyes. "Oh my God, I can't wait to introduce her to Ryan. And Toby! They're going to go crazy for her."

"Yes, but I suspect she'll find them too low-brow for her taste. I have to say, I'm really looking forward to getting to know her. Come on," I said, helping Rebecca to her feet. "Let's go get dinner."

\* \* \*

As it turned out, Lili had amazingly good taste. She showed up on the appointed day flanked by three movers who carried in load after load of boxes and furniture. Despite her promise to be "democratic," she had already gotten permission from Morgan to move out the communal furniture and replace it all with her own. I watched in awe as she transformed our living room. There was now a beautiful sectional sofa made of soft purple velvet under the window. In front of it stood a large, square, cherry-red coffee table on short chrome legs, which she topped with a geometric vase filled with assorted dried twigs and reeds. In the corner, where the worn-out plastic table had been, a mid-century dinette set of marbled grey Formica and chrome stood. And on the wall where the old, fake-wood entertainment center had held Tracy's television, there was now a low, black cabinet with blue accent lighting running along the bottom that supported a gigantic, high-definition TV.

I walked around taking pictures, texting them to Rebecca in New York, even though she had already given me the thumbs up on everything she'd seen so far. "You have remarkable stuff," I told Lili as she placed a multi-tiered floor lamp in the corner and bent to plug it in.

"Anything you don't like we can get rid of," she said as she straightened and turned on the lamp. Different colored lights shone through designs carved in the canisters while a central fixture cast a soft, white light over the room. "But I could tell immediately that you both had good taste and wouldn't mind. Rebecca comes from money, right?"

I was taken aback. "We don't really talk about it."

"Trust me, she's rolling in it," Lili said. "I got a look at her closet. In addition to the requisite UCSB logo wear, she's got several pieces from designers most people haven't heard of . . . yet. Her family's from New York?"

"Yes," I answered, a very strange feeling growing in the pit of my stomach.

"That explains it. Her mom probably picks stuff up and sends it here. She sure as hell didn't buy that Miha jacket at the mall."

Just then, my phone rang. "Excuse me," I said and wandered into the bedroom to take the call. It was Rebecca.

"Hey Bec, do you like all the furniture okay? Lili says we can . . . hey, what's up?" I suddenly felt the thick silence on the other end of the line.

"Christoph just left for the airport," she answered in a strained voice. "His parents called to say that his grandfather just passed away. It was very sudden. A heart attack, they think."

"Oh no, I'm so sorry! Was he really close to his grandfather?"

"They were very close when Christoph was young, although it sounds like they've become more estranged in the last several years."

"Poor Christoph! Oh man, what a nightmare. And he only just arrived in New York yesterday. I don't suppose he even had time to talk to your parents, then."

"No, he didn't. And I have to say that I'm relieved. He just told me to spend as much time with my family as I can, and then the driver came to pick him up and took him to JFK. He wouldn't even let me drop him off at the airport." Her voice quavered. "Ashlyn, I'm worried about him. I think this happening right after his accident might have been too much for him. He's really sensitive, despite how strong he is on the outside."

"I know what you mean. Sometimes I think he should have been an Empath. But I'm sure he'll be fine. He just needs to be with his family right now."

"So you don't think I should have insisted on going with him?" she asked.

"No, not at all. It's better that his family meet you under happy circumstances, not tragedy."

64

"That's what I was thinking, but then I felt like a bad girlfriend."

"Enough with the guilt already. Trust him to tell you what he needs. You can send his family flowers."

"Good idea." She breathed a sigh of relief. "Okay, I'm going to stop worrying about it now. I just feel so bad for him."

"Of course you do. But try to enjoy the rest of your time. Go out, have fun, do some shopping with your mom."

"I will. There's a trunk show tomorrow she wants to go to that's supposed to have some great bargains."

After we hung up, I thought about what Lili had said. I always knew Rebecca's family had money, but I never really thought about how much. Her parents seemed so down-to-earth, not ostentatious in the slightest, and I just assumed as human rights attorneys they didn't make a whole lot of money. But they had looked at properties in Santa Barbara when they came to visit, which, considering the cost of real estate in the area, was not something most people could even consider. I didn't know why I was giving the whole thing any thought at all, but for some reason, the thought of Rebecca being ultra-wealthy made me feel awkward.

As I was pondering this, I heard a knock at my door. My sister walked slowly into the room wearing dark sunglasses. She took them off to reveal puffy red eyes, and there were tears streaming down her face.

I jumped to my feet. "Laurel, what the . . . "

"It's that fucking bastard, Jason. He's been cheating on me."

I gasped, trying to control the rage that was building up inside of me. "No! You can't be serious! What happened?"

She wiped her nose on her sleeve. "It's true. I got him to admit the whole thing. Remember last Friday night when you and I went dancing? Jason ended up going out with his pretentious philosophy friends, and he hooked up with some artist."

"Oh my God, no."

"It gets worse," Laurel said, sitting down on my bed. "He ended up sneaking off and seeing her on Sunday when I was at Pilates, and then he saw her again on Tuesday. And now . . . you'll just love this . . . he says he's in love with her. I mean, what in the hell is he talking about? Who falls in love that fast?"

"Um, well . . . "

"Oh, you're different," she said, waving her hand dismissively. "You and Kai are soulmates and all that." She paused. "You don't think she's his soulmate, do you? Oh Ashlyn, what the hell am I going to do?"

She began sobbing loudly, and I pulled her into my arms. "Okay, first of all, Jason loves you. He's a cheating asshole at the moment, but he loves you. The question is: can you guys survive this kind of a betrayal? Are you ever going to be able to trust him again?"

She pulled back and looked searchingly into my eyes. "I just don't know."

"That's the first thing you have to figure out. Second, did he say he's still open to working things out with you and not seeing this person anymore?"

"He was really vague. He said he needed time to figure it out. And then he packed up all his clothes and left. I mean, all his clothes. I guess . . . I guess he actually moved out."

"Laurel, I'm so, so sorry." I held her for a while as she cried. I wanted to kill Jason. It took every ounce of strength I had to keep myself from flying out the door and hunting him down.

Finally, Laurel's sobs subsided. "I need a drink. Can we go to the tavern or something?"

"Sure. Go wash your face, and let's go down to the café and get something to eat first."

She got heavily to her feet and trudged into my bathroom. I quickly changed my tear-soaked, mascara-smudged shirt, and then we headed out into the living room.

What we saw stopped us dead in our tracks. There was Lili, surrounded by her beautiful furniture like a queen bee in her hive, making out with Jason on the purple velvet couch.

## Chapter Eight: Entanglements

My phone rang just as I returned to the apartment. "How is she doing?" Mom's voice was thick with worry.

I sat heavily on the sofa but sprang to my feet again when I remembered it as the scene of the crime. Pacing the room seemed a safer occupation at the moment. "About as well as you'd expect. I tried to stay with her, but she wouldn't have it."

"Poor Laurel. I never would have thought this of Jason. Just goes to show you never can tell."

"No," I sighed. "You can't. All you can do is hope, I guess. But I doubt after this she'll be able to trust anyone."

"Sure she will," Lili said as she crossed the living room to the kitchen.

"Did I just hear that slut roommate of yours?" Mom's voice rang out from my phone, definitely loud enough for Lili to hear. I cringed, but Lili seemed completely unfazed.

"I prefer to think of myself as a volunteer sex worker," Lili said. "Many people simply crave intimacy, to unleash their kundalini energy in a safe, non-judgmental—"

I hurried to my room and shut the door, but Mom was already ranting. "You are moving out. I don't care if you signed a lease, you're not letting Kai anywhere near that woman."

I laughed. "A year ago I would have agreed with you, but I know Kai wouldn't fall prey to her. And besides, Jason's the guilty party here. Lili didn't even know he was in a relationship. He was the one sneaking around."

"A drug addict one year and a sex addict the next," Mom said in disgust. "They're doing a wonderful job of finding you roommates."

"Can we get back to Laurel? What are we going to do?"

"You know how she is," Mom said, sounding exasperated. "She likes to be alone when she's upset. Just keep checking in on her and make sure you get her out of the house. Take her to the beach, the movies—anything to keep her from chewing on this, or it'll drive her nuts."

After we hung up, I sat in front of the mirror, staring at my reflection, absent-mindedly turning over my figurine of the goddess Fuchi in my fingers like a worry bead. Laurel was now living one of my worst nightmares, and yet for some reason, I wasn't freaking out. I remembered the time when Maggie found out that her boyfriend was having a major affair behind her back. It seemed to turn all our lives upside down, and for weeks afterward, I was totally paranoid that Todd was going to cheat on me.

But this time, instead of all my old insecurities surfacing, I was oddly calm. I even felt a little sorry for Jason for screwing everything up so badly. Lili clearly had no intention of having a relationship with him or anyone, and although casual kundalini sex or whatever the hell they were doing would seem awesome for a little while, I was sure it wouldn't be long before he missed Laurel. Michael's face suddenly popped unbidden into my mind, and as I remembered the last dream I'd had about him, my cheeks flushed. Obviously, I

69

had a much better understanding of temptation than I'd ever had before.

I put on my cycling gear and tore out of the apartment, hoping I could burn off some of my pent-up energy, and possibly outrun some of the unwelcome feelings I was battling. I raced along the trails, hardly seeing the ocean, focusing completely on the path ahead of me as I pumped the pedals harder and harder. The sky darkened to a deeper hue, and the sunlight gleamed more brightly on my bike's frame, when suddenly I had the disturbing sensation that I wasn't moving anymore, that I was stationary and the world was spinning below me. It was as if I were on a huge treadmill that would react instantly to my movements. I slowed my pace, and the world rolled more slowly. I turned my handlebars to the right, and the world shifted underneath me to accommodate my change in direction. I hit the brakes and stopped, panting hard. I moved forward a few inches, and I felt the earth slip below me in response. I was going nowhere; the world was the only thing actually moving. I found myself unable to shake the odd sensation, and aside from being deeply unsettling, it made it very hard to keep riding. What the hell was going on?

I was just starting to panic for real when I heard my name. I turned and saw Toby biking toward me.

"Hey," he said, glancing down at my tires as he came to a stop next to me. "Something wrong?"

"No, at least . . . no, it's all good." I looked around. "But now that you mention it, does anything seem kind of odd to you?"

He cocked his head at me. "Odd in what way?"

"Never mind. I think I got too much of an endorphin rush from my ride."

"Are you okay? Do you want me to go get my car?"

"No, I'm good. Thanks, Toby. Maybe just ride back with me."

I tentatively stepped on the pedal and pushed forward. I was still having the unshakable sensation that I wasn't moving, that the world was moving underneath me, but having Toby next to me made me feel more normal. He started telling me about his trip to Las Vegas with Ryan, and soon I was laughing and forgot all about my bizarre world-as-treadmill experience.

In hindsight, it's not something I should have forgotten so quickly.

Over the next couple of days, I spent a lot of time with Laurel. Jason came over once, and they got into a screaming fight that ended with her throwing a plate at his head and him slamming the front door so hard I thought the windows would shatter. She alternated between fits of rage, in which she stormed around her apartment yelling about what bastards men were, and crying jags that ended in her sitting numbly in front of the television, staring blankly at the screen without seeing anything. I cooked for her and got her to keep eating enough to survive, but I was really worried. And at the same time, I kept asking myself whether all of this was necessary. I mean, there was no doubt that what Jason did was unacceptable. But was it the fact that he had sex with someone else or the fact that he lied about it and sneaked around behind her back? I knew that my heavy crush on Michael made no difference at all in how I felt about Kai, so would it really have to be the end of our relationship if he and I hooked up one lonely night when Kai and Marlowe were on the road, as long as they knew about it in advance? I didn't see why it had to be such a big deal, until I thought about Kai and Marlowe doing the same thing, at which point I actually gagged.

These questions were still weighing heavily on my mind when I got home on the third night and found Lili doing yoga in the living room. I didn't think she had that great a body— she was too boyish, in my opinion—but she had an unbelievable confidence and sexuality about her, and I could see why guys would be into her. I sat and watched her for a moment before she spoke.

"How's Laurel?" she asked.

"A mess." I sat on the couch, and she turned toward me as she moved into a position I recognized as Triangle pose from my short-lived attempt at starting a yoga practice.

"I'm really sorry about all this. Sucks that he didn't have the balls to do the right thing."

I looked at her with new interest. "You would have wanted him to stop pursuing you out of respect for his relationship with Laurel?"

"No, I think he should have been man enough to tell Laurel that he needed to be with someone else for a few nights." She switched into Proud Warrior pose, staring over her outstretched arm toward the other side of the room.

"From the sound of it, he was thinking of more than a few nights. He claims to be falling in love with you."

"That's because he's not being honest with himself, either. A couple of fantastically hot nights of sex aren't the same thing as love."

"Have you ever been in love?" I asked doubtfully.

"Only once, but it was enough to know the difference." She sat in a full Lotus pose, with her legs crossed and her feet resting high up on her thighs. It made her look like something between a princess and a pretzel. "For the most part, falling in love isn't worth the trouble. Emotional entanglements are too disruptive. I don't know anyone who can withstand the maelstrom of falling in love without losing themselves and succumbing to the urge to waste their time daydreaming about the person and worrying about all the different ways the person might hurt them. It goes beyond all logic and reason." She hoisted herself up on her hands so that her crossed legs were suspended in the air.

"That may be, but I wouldn't trade it for anything. Kai is the best thing that ever happened to me. Sure, there have been a lot of struggles, but I've grown more from working through those issues in the last eighteen months than I did in years of dating someone who wasn't right for me."

"That's great. But there's going to come a time when you need to be apart, and it would be a whole lot nicer if that day didn't ruin your happiness and well-being. Look at your sister. Was it really worth it?"

She got up slowly and crossed the floor to the kitchen, where she drank a tall glass of water before grabbing a banana and heading back toward her room.

"Even if I do end up like Laurel some day," I said before she reached her door, "it will have been worth it. Every minute of it." She turned and looked back at me with a perplexed expression, and I knew she could tell that I meant it. She shrugged and headed into her room. But in that moment, I figured out two things: one, that no matter what happened, even if Kai did end up sleeping with someone else, I would forgive him and move on; and two, I would do everything I could to make him trust me so that he'd never feel the need to lie to me again.

As I got up to return to my room, my phone rang. It was Rebecca.

"Hey, Bec, how's—" But my words were cut short by the sound of her sobbing on the other end. At first I couldn't make out what she was saying. But when I finally did understand her, I simply couldn't believe it.

"What do you mean he's not coming back?" I asked.

"Please, Ashlyn, oh please," she wailed. "I don't think I can stand it. I don't know how I'm going to survive this." The phone dropped, and suddenly I heard her mother's voice on the line.

"Ashlyn, this is Susan. Can you come to New York?"

"To New York? Um, yeah . . . yes, I can do that. I'll—"

"I'll have a car pick you up in half an hour and take you to LAX. You'll be able to get right onto the next plane. I'll have a ticket waiting for you at the counter."

"Half an hour? Mrs. Epstein—"

"Susan, please."

"Susan, what is going on? What does Rebecca mean Christoph isn't coming back?"

"That's what we'd all like to find out," she replied. "But in the meantime, Rebecca desperately needs her best friend." Her voice was strained to the point of nearly cracking.

"Okay," I said. "I'll be ready in half an hour."

I hung up and hurried into the bedroom to start packing while my mind raced. What in the hell was going on? First Laurel, now Rebecca? And oh crap, what was I going to tell Laurel? I was supposed to take her to the beach tomorrow to get her out of the house, and instead I'd be in New York. New York! God, I'd always wanted to go there, and now here I was about to be whisked off to the airport to a waiting airline ticket—I hoped that meant I didn't have to pay for it, then immediately felt guilty for thinking about my budget at a time like that—but I was going there because my best friend was on the edge because her boyfriend (no, *fiancé*, I reminded myself) had suddenly decided to stay in Germany. I sat for a moment and noticed my hands were shaking. It was all too much, but I didn't have time to fall apart. There would be plenty of time to freak out later.

## Chapter Nine: The Penthouse

"Good to see you, Ashlyn. I'm glad you could come." Rebecca's father, Bob, shook my hand warmly and led me toward the waiting town car. I noticed that the creases in his forehead seemed more pronounced than the last time I'd seen him. "How was your flight?"

"I actually managed to sleep a bit. Which is good, because I can't believe it's already morning. It's still three A.M. my time." I stifled a yawn as I looked at my watch. "So how is she doing?"

"Not well at all. She's barely eating." He ran his hand through his thinning hair as we climbed into the back seat. The driver pulled smoothly away from the curb, and I settled into the comfortable leather seats. The car felt toasty warm after the chilly morning air, and I instantly felt like falling asleep again. But I was way too wired for that.

"So what happened exactly?" I asked. "And what does she mean he's not coming back?"

"She got an email from him yesterday saying he decided to stay in Germany and that she shouldn't contact him again. She tried to call him, but his phone number had been disconnected, and his emails started bouncing right after that." He started talking quickly, as if he had been holding everything in until this moment. "I've just never seen her like this. She's never been boy crazy before. She dated one or two boys in high school, but it was never anything serious. And now suddenly her life is over because some . . . some German decides he wants to go home? And there's nothing her mother or I can say to make her feel any better. We've tried explaining that she's young, she's got lots of time to meet other boys."

I cringed. "You, um, you didn't actually say that to her, did you?"

"Well, we were just trying to reason with her."

"Mr. Epstein—"

"Please call me Bob."

"Bob, it's better not to try to talk her out of being in love with Christoph. I know both of them pretty well, and he would never have disappeared like this unless something is really wrong. What Rebecca needs right now is for us to help her keep up hope that he is coming back after he sorts through whatever happened and not let her believe that he got cold feet."

Bob narrowed his eyes at me. "Cold feet? What exactly are you saying?"

A sickening wave of guilt washed over me. "Um, you know, about their relationship."

He continued to peer at me. "Are you saying they were engaged?"

It was like all the air had been sucked out of the car. Holy shit, how could I be so stupid as to let that slip? Trying not to panic, I cracked the window a bit and let the cold air blast me in the face to calm me down. "What matters is that we support Rebecca through this very real crisis. It's not just a crush. They really do love each other. You must have noticed that even in the short time you met him."

He looked straight ahead and said nothing for a while. Finally, he let out a big sigh. "As you said, let's just get her out of crisis, and then her mother and I are going to have a long talk with her about the choices she's making."

I bit my lip. Here I'd flown all the way to New York to help Rebecca through the worst time of her life, and so far all I'd ended up doing was betraying her confidence. It didn't bode well for the rest of the visit. But my guilt was quickly overshadowed by the sight of Manhattan rising in the distance. Seeing that skyline for the first time was like magic, as if a movie set had suddenly become real.

"Are we going into the city?" I asked. "I thought you lived in White Plains."

"We're staying uptown at my mother's flat. Rebecca has her own room there. She lived there when she was attending high school in the city."

"Rebecca didn't live with you in high school?"

"No. We saw her on weekends, of course, and on Wednesdays we would come into the city and take her to dinner. When we weren't out of town, that is." I wondered why Rebecca had never mentioned it before. I had always just assumed that she'd lived with her parents up until college, but when I thought about it, all the stories she told me took place in Manhattan.

As we headed into the city, I could feel the buzz of energy vibrating all around me. The sidewalks were crowded with people rushing along as they swung briefcases and talked on cell phones. Bike messengers weaved in and out of traffic, which was a sea of black town cars and yellow taxis. The buildings rose up around us, swallowing the sky, as if we were in a canyon of brick, steel, and glass. It felt like we were suddenly in the very center of the universe, and everything else in existence rotated around this one small island.

We drove farther uptown until we reached a very posh neighborhood. As we passed a woman in a leopard coat and high black heels who was so tall and thin she must have been a supermodel, I glanced down at my jeans and t-shirt that I'd thrown on in my race to get to the airport. Even the dogs here looked better groomed than I did. I hoped we could slip into Rebecca's building without too many of her neighbors seeing me. If not, I could always pretend to be the new maid.

We turned onto a side street lined with trees and stopped in front of a building made of pale grey stone with a white awning on which the street number was spelled out in fancy, black script letters. The driver hopped out and opened my door. I felt a little ridiculous as he helped me out of the car, but I took a deep breath and tried not to be intimidated. Bob grabbed my suitcase out of the trunk, nodded in return to the doorman's greeting, and led me inside to the immaculate marble lobby.

When we stepped off the elevators into the penthouse suite, I realized that Theresa, wealthy as she may have been, was a pauper compared to Rebecca's family. It was way beyond anything I had imagined. The light marble entryway led into a beautiful living room with rich walnut floors, pale lavender walls, and four huge windows with sweeping views of the Manhattan skyline. Over the mantle was a portrait of Rebecca and her parents at the beach, all dressed in white and barefoot, laughing merrily as they walked on the sand and the wind danced in their hair. It looked as if it were taken a few years ago, before she came to college. Before she became a Soterian. I got a lump in my throat seeing Rebecca looking so young and happy.

Quick footsteps approached, and I turned to see Susan hurrying toward us. "Ashlyn, thank goodness you're here. Rebecca's awake, you can go right in and see her." She took my arm and steered me down the narrow hallway as she lowered her voice to barely more than a whisper. "She's getting worse. You've got to snap her out of this. Do whatever it takes. Talk about happy things back in Santa Barbara: your life there, your friends. How much she loves the school. Anything to take her mind off Christoph." She spoke in even tones, but her eyes were filled with anguish, and I felt a pain coming from her that was like a very old wound had been recently reopened.

"You've experienced heartbreak before?" I asked softly.

Susan paused in front of a door. "Yes, of course. We all have."

"Then you know you can't just be talked out of how you feel." I touched her lightly on the arm and walked into Rebecca's bedroom, closing the door behind me.

The room was gigantic, about the size of our entire apartment. In one corner was a large desk that held a computer with a huge monitor. Two large, comfy-looking chairs were surrounded by floor-to-ceiling shelves crammed with books. And in the far corner was a huge bed with a canopy over it. It all reminded me of the room I'd fallen in love with during my escape from Bennicort's mansion, and for a moment I tried to imagine how Rebecca must have felt going from this amazing space to sharing a tiny room with me, a complete stranger.

But my thoughts were interrupted by a movement at the window at the far end of the room. Through the dim light, I saw Rebecca sitting on a window seat that overlooked the city. She turned and looked at me with such sad, sunken eyes that I had to hold back a gasp. She made a little sound, and I was nearly knocked back from the unbearable pain emanating from her. I steadied myself, raced over to where she was sitting, and threw my arms around her.

"Oh Bec, I'm so sorry," I said as she clung to me and started to cry. I held her tightly and stroked her hair as she wept. "It's okay, we're going to figure this out. Don't worry," I whispered.

She pulled back and looked at me with tears streaming down her face. "Thank you so much for being here. I don't know what I'm going to do, Ashlyn. I can't stand it. I lost him once, and now he's gone for good. I feel like I can't live through this again."

"There is no way in hell he's gone for good," I insisted. "This is Christoph we're talking about. Christoph, for God's sake! The guy who worships the ground you walk on. Who dug through snow for two days because he needed to live for you." She winced at the memory, and another stab of pain shot through me. "Trust me, something is really, really wrong. He's freaking out about something and needs some time to figure it out. Have you managed to talk to him at all?"

She wiped her eyes on her sleeve. "No," she said. "His emails bounced, and his phone is disconnected. I did a search for his family's phone number, and I thought I found the right name and town, but when I told them who I was, they said there was no Christoph there."

I stared at her, trying to make sense of what she was telling me. Why would Christoph suddenly decide to stay in Germany and break things off with Rebecca so completely? He had to have snapped. Or was it something more sinister than that? Rage began to build inside of me.

"I know what you're thinking," Rebecca said. "And I don't see how this could have anything to do with Deimos."

I jumped to my feet. "Think about it, though! Our Sentry is gone under mysterious circumstances, which has caused our Empath to be completely out of commission, and our Scout to go try to help figure this out. We've lost three quarters of our unit to this bullshit. Who knows what Deimos might be doing while we're here?"

"It won't work," Rebecca said, shaking her head sadly. "I know you're trying to get me to rally by talking about our mission, but it won't work. My life is over. I can't go back to Santa Barbara. And I can't be a Soterian anymore. I'm sorry." She broke down into tears and buried her head in her knees. I rubbed her back and tried to think what my next move would be. I was absolutely certain that Deimos was behind this, and I needed to get her back with our unit so we could figure out what was going on.

"Rebecca, believe me, I know what you're feeling. And it's killing me inside. But I don't believe for one second that this is over. I think Christoph needs our help again, and the only way to fight for him is to be with our unit. We have to try!"

She looked up at me and rested her cheek on her knee. "I'm so tired," she said. "I can't fight anymore. I just want to die."

"Well, the first thing you have to do is eat and then get some sleep. We're not deciding anything until you've taken care of yourself.

"I can't eat. Everything tastes like ash."

I raised my eyebrow at her. "Rebecca, we're in New York. You can't tell me there's not one dish in this city that will tempt you. Come on, what was your favorite place to eat when you were a kid? Some place with good comfort food." She stared back at me dully. "Help me out," I said. "I've never been here and have no idea where to go. And I have to say, I'm pretty damn hungry after traveling all night. Is there someplace that has good waffles?"

I felt something stir in her. "I'm sorry. I shouldn't have asked you to come all the way across the country."

"Don't make me kick your ass. You're my best friend in the entire world, and I love you. And I've always, always wanted to come to New York. How many times have we talked about coming here together? You were going to show me all these cool places you know. Wasn't there a gallery you said I'd love? Do they serve waffles?"

A shadow of a smile crossed her lips. "I know what you're trying to do. And even though it's not working, I really appreciate it." She took my hand. "Thank you. I don't think I could have made it through another hour without you." She took a deep breath. "I can't go back to Santa Barbara, Ashlyn. I just can't face being there without him."

"We don't have to talk about that right now. All we need to do is get me some waffles."

She rolled her eyes slightly. "One step at a time, is that it?"

"That's exactly it. We're just going to take care of what's right in front of us, nothing else. And right now what's in front of us is—"

"Waffles, yes, I got it." She got slowly to her feet, and I steered her toward her bathroom.

"Wash your face while I pick out something for you to wear." I walked over to her closet and flipped on the light. I stopped in my tracks. I was standing at the entrance to a walk-in closet that was larger than our bedroom. Racks and racks of shirts, pants, dresses, skirts, and jackets lined the left edge of the room, while the right side was filled with shelves of shoes. In the center was a large dresser that I guessed was stuffed with sweaters and underwear. At the far end of the room was a padded bench and a full-length mirror that showed your reflection from three angles. "Um, Bec? Maybe you'd better give me a hand. Do you just have a pair of comfy sweats or something?"

She walked up behind me and looked blankly at her clothes. "I used to love shopping," she said. "It was so much fun to find cute things to add to my wardrobe, especially when I found them on sale. A quirky pair of shoes that would go just right with jeans and a sweater. Or a new jacket that could make a plain skirt look completely different. I can't believe something so stupid seemed fun before. They're just clothes."

Rebecca reached out to switch off the light, but I stopped her. "What used to be your favorite thing to wear? The outfit that felt the most like home to you?"

She picked up a faded pair of jeans and pulled a royal blue sweater out of a drawer.

"And the quirky shoes?" I prompted.

She slowly crossed the room to the shoe rack and picked up a pair of worn, black leather boots embroidered with patterns in yellow thread and covered in silver studs.

I nodded appreciatively. "Perfect. Hurry up and get dressed. I'm starving. I'll meet you in the hall in thirty seconds."

I walked out of her room and found her parents in the hallway, looking nervously at me. "Well?"

"You're right, she's in really bad shape. But at least she's getting dressed and we're going out to get something to eat." They looked relieved, but I raised my hand. "We just need to take this one step at a time. So for now, it would probably be best if we didn't talk about her relationship with Christoph or her future plans or anything, okay?"

"Agreed," Susan said. "Let's just get through today." Bob nodded in agreement just as Rebecca opened the door. She was wearing dark sunglasses.

"Mom, Dad," she said. "I'm going to take Ashlyn out to get something to eat. We'll be back later."

"Okay, sweetheart, take your time. We love you." Susan kissed Rebecca on the forehead, and Bob put his hand on her shoulder. She tried to smile, which came out as more of a grimace, before leading me down the hall and out into the streets of New York.

## Chapter Ten: The Message in the Gallery

"I've been to some cool galleries in San Francisco, but this is unreal."

I ambled through the gallery, visually drinking in everything I saw. The walls were lined with art of all genres and sizes. Huge abstract paintings hung next to still-life portraits, which were bordered by tiny etchings in large frames. Woven baskets stood on the pale, hardwood floor and were filled with gigantic floral arrangements. A long skylight flooded the room with natural light, giving the rooms a sense of openness and space. It was peaceful and inspiring all at once.

Equally inspiring were the prices. I didn't see a single piece of art for less than twelve thousand dollars. It made Theresa's gallery seem like a sidewalk sale. But then again, she dealt mostly in folk art, and from the artist profiles posted on the wall, it appeared that all these artists lived in New York. I couldn't imagine how they sold enough art to support themselves living in the city, even at those prices.

Rebecca walked along with me, appearing only vaguely interested. She had said almost nothing during breakfast, content to stir a cup of coffee she never drank and to watch me devour my waffles. I did manage to talk her into eating a few pieces of my fruit, but nothing more. I had no idea how I was going to get her to move out of her depression and start coping with what had happened.

"Hey Bec, look at this one." I pointed out a beautiful scene with mountains and a lonely cottage perched at the top of one of the taller peaks.

Rebecca eyed it for a moment, then turned away. "It looks like a picture Christoph showed me of his home."

"He lives on top of a mountain?"

"No, they have a vacation home in the mountains. He used to stay there every summer."

"Maybe he's there now. Maybe he went to think things through. He's had a hell of a time lately, what with almost dying in the snow and then his grandfather passing away."

"And asking me to marry him. Apparently that was the thing that pushed him over the edge." Rebecca's face looked sunken and pale.

"Is that what you think? Bec, that's ridiculous. You were the one thing that kept him going. You know that. I don't know how many times I have to tell you this, but even though you know Christoph better than anyone, you're not in any shape to judge his actions right now. I know him pretty well, too, and I can tell you one hundred percent that something bad has happened to him to make him act this way, and it has nothing to do with you."

"Then why won't he talk to me? If I'm so important to him, why the hell did he break up with me? Can you explain that?" Her voice rose, and a few patrons turned to look at us. "One day he was pledging his undying love to me and was going to ask my parents for permission to marry me, and the next day he changes his email and phone number and says he never wants to see me again!"

I put my arm around her. "I know. I know! It makes absolutely no sense at all."

She pulled away from me. "Then stop telling me I'm crazy and don't understand what he's going through. I know exactly what he's going through. He went home, saw his family and his friends and realized that his real life is there. And that I have no place in that world."

"But why not? That makes no sense at all. Even if he did realize he loves Germany and wants to stay there, why wouldn't he try to convince you to come there? Do you really think he'd break things off so abruptly because he's afraid of asking you to move to Germany? That just doesn't sound like him."

Rebecca sat heavily on a bench and pulled at her hair. "None of it sounds like him. I just can't figure it out."

I sat next to her. "I can't either. But believe me, we're going to get to the bottom of this. Just like you didn't give up when he disappeared under the snow, you've got to be strong now and not give up just because he disappeared to Germany. It had to be something as strong as an avalanche—metaphorically speaking."

She gazed out the window, and I was about to convince her that we should go take a walk in Central Park, when suddenly something on the wall caught my eye. Hanging in a small, gilded frame was an oil painting of a bright, crimson poppy in the snow. It was painted in an abstract style, the flower a slash of paint across the speckled frost. But what was most impressive about it was that the scene was moving. Snow was actually falling in the picture, collecting in the corners of the frame, and the poppy was twisting slowly, as if it were trying to free itself from the snow's icy embrace.

I stood and moved toward the painting, amazed. Was it a hologram? I glanced up at the ceiling to see whether there was a projector, but I didn't see anything. I looked back at the painting to try to figure it out, but now it was totally still.

What the hell?

Maybe it was an optical illusion. I took a step back, but it wasn't moving. Rebecca looked up at me curiously. "What is it?" she asked.

An explosion of sound shot through the room. Rebecca and I fell to the floor as shattered glass burst from the front window, and the gallery filled with screams from the customers. My heart was hammering as I looked up and saw a short, stocky man, completely naked, standing where the front display window had been. He was waving his bloody arms wildly, glass sticking out of his hands and face, his mouth working furiously as if he were trying to find words that simply wouldn't come. He let out a shriek that pierced the air and then collapsed in the broken glass.

Rebecca was the first to her feet. She sprang toward the man and quickly knelt next to him, checking for a pulse. "Call nine-one-one!" she shouted. I glanced toward the counter and saw the sales woman picking up the phone and dialing. I ran to Rebecca's side and watched as she quickly looked him over. He was bleeding heavily. "Get the first aid kit," she barked. I ran to the back of the gallery, where several terrified-looking women were standing, their hands over their gaping mouths or clutching their chests.

"Where's your first aid kit?" I demanded of the woman behind the counter. She hung up the phone and ran into a back room, reappearing a moment later carrying a white plastic box with a red cross on it. I grabbed the kit and hurried back to the front of the store, where Rebecca was waiting. She grabbed it from me, pulled on a pair of gloves, ripped open a thick gauze pad and immediately applied pressure to one of the spots where he was bleeding the worst.

"It's bad," she said, still staring at the man. "What the hell happened?"

"He's probably schizophrenic," I guessed. "Or on drugs."

"Stay back from the blood," Rebecca warned. "There isn't another pair of gloves."

The sound of sirens filled the air, and moments later two paramedics arrived. I had a vague sense of déjà vu. It seemed like I'd seen more ambulances and hospitals in the last twelve months than I'd seen in my entire life.

Rebecca quickly moved aside as the paramedics moved in. She filled them in, and they worked quickly, one of them pressing thick cotton pads against the wounds while the other strapped the man to a gurney. Just as they started to move him toward the door, his eyes snapped open, and he locked his gaze on Rebecca.

"Don't run! Don't run!" he implored her, his eyes wild. "You must go back!"

Rebecca stared at him, aghast, as the paramedics wheeled him out of the gallery.

I approached her slowly, picking my way over the broken glass, which crunched loudly under my feet in the silence that now filled the room. I put my hand tentatively on Rebecca's shoulder. "He may have been crazy, but he sure seemed to have the right message for you."

She turned and looked at me, puzzled. "What do you mean?"

"It doesn't matter that you lost your powers. You just saved that man's life. Nobody in this gallery knew what to do. Not even me. My Alchemist powers never activated, and I bet it was because you had the situation totally under control. The Soterians need you, right now, but more importantly, your future patients need you. You have to come back to school and finish your degree so you can go to med school and be the person you were born to be."

The dullness that had covered her face like a mask was gone, and there was a small spark in her deep brown eyes. "We can't do this without you," I continued, then put my hands on her shoulders. "I can't do this without you. Please come home, Bec."

She turned for a moment, watching the ambulance pull away, then took a deep breath. "Okay."

"Okay?"

She nodded. I searched her face, which was still so full of pain, but the spark in her eyes was definitely back. I gave her a long hug before we turned and picked our way over the shards of glass. As we walked out of the gallery, I glanced back at the picture of the poppy. It was a still life once again. Jet lag can do funny things, I decided, and followed Rebecca outside.

As we waited in the terminal for our flight to Los Angeles, I called Laurel, cringing as I dialed. She had been less than empathetic about my jetting off to New York, despite the fact that Rebecca's crisis was actually far worse than her own at the moment. But when I called her, she seemed to be calmer.

"How are you doing?" I asked tentatively.

"I'm okay," she sighed. "But there's no way I can concentrate on school right now. I need to get the hell out of here, so I'm going to stay at Dad's for a week."

"Spending time with Dad should definitely take your mind off things, but is he really okay with you missing school?"

"He wasn't at first, but Evelyn shut him up. She at least remembers what it's like to have your heart ripped out by an asshole. Plus, they're going out of town, so I'm going to housesit for them. I need some quiet time to think, and they need someone to watch the house."

"Are you sure you're going to be okay by yourself in that big house?" I panicked immediately after asking the question. What if she asked me to come stay with her? I'd have to say no, but how could I after I just flew to New York for Rebecca?

"I'll be fine. I really want time alone."

"Okay," I said, trying not to breathe the sigh of relief too audibly. "But be sure to go spend time with Mom, too. She always helps."

"Is Rebecca doing any better?"

"She's hanging in there. She'll be much better once we can get in touch with Christoph."

"Don't hold your breath," Laurel spat. "Men are pigs, and he's no exception. I don't care what his problem is. He doesn't deserve Rebecca, and she should get over him as fast as possible."

"Yes, well, I don't think I'll pass that message along just yet. Take care, Laurel."

I hung up and put my phone back in my bag, wishing life weren't so complicated. I turned to Rebecca and found her looking at me with a strange expression.

"I'm sorry about all this," she said. "I know you feel pulled in a million directions. You should be with Laurel."

"Rebecca, please shut up. I need to be with you, with our unit. We need to find Christoph."

Rebecca looked sad. "Even if we do find him, what makes you think he'll come back?"

I put my arm around her shoulders. "Because if he tries to resist, I'll rearrange his face."

Rebecca gazed at me and then let out a small laugh. It sounded raspy and hollow, like she'd forgotten how. I felt a lump in my throat and was very happy to hear the announcement over the loud speaker that our flight was boarding. As we gathered up our stuff, I swore under my breath that I would kill Christoph for doing this to Rebecca, but a wave of guilt washed over me. What if something was really wrong with him? I swayed slightly and had to grab onto a chair to stop myself from falling over.

"Ashlyn?" Rebecca asked, looking back at me with deep concern.

I ran my hand over my forehead, which had broken out into a sweat. "I'm okay. Just stood up too fast." I took a deep breath and followed her onto the plane, wondering whether I was just exhausted from the last few days or was sensing something from Christoph all the way across the ocean.

When we touched down in Los Angeles, a car was waiting to take us back to Santa Barbara. As we climbed into the back seat, Rebecca asked the driver to take the Pacific Coast Highway. We settled into the comfortable leather seats and both sighed heavily.

"I feel like I've been gone a really long time," she mused.

"I know exactly what you mean. It's good to be home. Home . . . you ever wonder where you'll end up? Where home will be?"

Rebecca looked pensive for a moment. "I can't see myself anywhere but New York. How about you?"

I glanced out the window as Santa Monica Bay shimmered in the early evening sunlight. "Yeah, I could see living in New York. But I don't know. San Francisco will always feel like my city, even though I've never actually lived in the city itself. Speaking of which," I said, turning away from the window. "What was it like living away from your parents during high school? I always assumed when you came to Santa Barbara, that was your first time away from home."

"It was, really. My grandmother's place was as much a home to me as our house in White Plains. And my parents were always traveling, so I was used to not seeing them every night at the dinner table."

"That must have been kind of shitty at times. Didn't you feel sort of abandoned?"

She looked pensive. "I don't know. I guess when I moved in with my Nana I felt a little more stable. She travels, too, but not nearly as much as my parents."

We were silent for much of the rest of the drive. As the car wound its way along the coast, I thought about Rebecca's childhood. I always thought of myself as the insecure one, but this episode with Christoph had affected her in a somewhat surprising way, and I started to wonder whether she had some of the same abandonment issues I had.

When the car finally turned onto our street, I felt a surge of excitement. We were home, and Kai would be waiting to see me. But then I remembered that Christoph wasn't there, and I couldn't just go racing over to The Manor to see Kai. Just as I was deliberating how best to navigate this mess, my phone rang.

"Ashlyn, it's Theresa."

"Hey, Theresa, how are things?"

"Not good at all. You're home now?"

"Just arrived." I glanced over at Rebecca, whose eyes had clouded over as soon as we pulled into the parking lot. She was staring straight ahead, as if she was doing everything she could not to look toward The Manor.

"Good," Theresa said, "because we need to see you both right away. Meet us at John's in half an hour. And yes," she said before I could ask, "bring Kai."

"Um, do you think we could maybe get settled in a bit first? Rebecca is—"

"I'm fine," Rebecca cut in. "Tell her we'll drop off our stuff and be right over."

"—ready to get right back into things, apparently." I hung up. "Are you sure?" I asked Rebecca.

"No, but I can't wait until I am." She opened our front door and stopped short. I peered past her and remembered that our living room had been completely redecorated since she was last here. "Everything's changed, hasn't it?" she mused as she slowly walked through the living room and inspected Lili's furniture.

"As far as I can tell, change is the only thing you can ever really count on. C'mon, let's get over to John's."

## Chapter Eleven: Epidemic

"The situation is out of hand," Theresa began. She was pacing around like a drill sergeant while Kai, Michael, Rebecca, and I watched and listened in silence. John stood off to the side, his chin cradled in one hand, his eyes fixed on the floor and the ever-deepening crease in his brow turning to a furrow. "The epidemic has spread like wildfire, and Kenji is killing himself trying to find a cure. Our other Sentry is hiding in Germany and won't answer our phone calls. He might as well have fallen into a bottomless pit. Again."

I felt a wave of sorrow emanate from Rebecca, and I gently touched her on the arm, sending healing energy into her. Michael's heartbeat sped up at Theresa's comment, but when I glanced over at him, his face was like stone. I admired his self-control, because I was pretty sure my face was making it clear I wanted to kill Theresa right then. I was grateful that she didn't look my way as she continued her tirade.

"Raina is distracted by problems with the city over the permit for her store. Jesse and Paul are quarreling about their future. Claire is consumed by her schoolwork and internship, and you," she said, whirling around to face Rebecca, "are almost useless in your current state. You can barely walk erect, let alone heal anyone."

"Maybe Michael should break your nose so we can test her," I blurted out.

"Ashlyn," John growled. "You will not disrespect Theresa again. Do I make myself clear?"

I felt my face flush with anger. "I'm sorry. But, I would appreciate it if we could get to the point of this lecture, as I really don't see how insulting us is going to solve anything."

"What do you propose, then?" Theresa's eyes flashed at me. "People are being hospitalized all across the country, and you're unable to do anything because you're so caught up with school and boyfriends and trivial matters. You are *Soterians*," she hissed. "You should be able to handle this."

I was about to speak when Rebecca interrupted. "She's right," she said. "The only reason I came back was to do my job as an Empath. It's the only thing that matters now. John, what do you think we should do?"

Theresa looked impatiently at John, and I realized that most of her anger was actually directed at him. It had to be hard to try to lead the two units together when their leadership styles were so different. She was all about taking action and giving orders, while he preferred to take a more passive role and let us find our own way. She was demanding; he was supportive. And yet they were both extremely wise and powerful Mentors.

John lifted his gaze to Rebecca, and they locked eyes for a few moments. "I think we need to play to our strengths," he began. "We're fractured and all going in different directions right now. But instead of fighting it, let's divide and conquer. Paul can work with Kenji to gather data and try to find the source of the outbreak. Jesse can do recon with Claire at the hospitals to see what information they might be overlooking or not sharing. Michael and Kai can focus on trying to track down Christoph. Raina can focus on solving her business problems, and Ashlyn can help Rebecca recover." He turned to Theresa. "And you and I can do everything in our own power to assist them."

His words were forceful, and yet there was a hint of defeat in his voice. It reminded me of something, but before I could put my finger on it, Theresa cut in.

"Very well. I'm driving back to San Francisco in an hour and will speak with the others." She glared at John. "Let's hope you're right."

And with that, she turned and walked out of the house, slamming the door behind her. Calm settled over the room for a moment, as if we were all catching our breath. Theresa could really suck the air out of the room when she was pissed off.

Kai reached out and took my hand. "We should look up the names of the neighbors around Christoph's parent's house. Maybe I can reach one of them and find out what's going on. But first," he said, standing up. "I'm afraid I have to go to band practice."

"Now?" hissed Michael, his eyes fixed coldly on Kai.

"We've got to get this last track finished," Kai explained. His phone beeped, and he glanced down, looking distracted. "It's only for a few hours. You can do some research while I'm gone, and I'll make phone calls later tonight, which will be first thing in the morning in Germany."

"You're going to call Germany?" Rebecca asked. "What if they don't speak English?"

"I took German in high school. I should remember enough to get by." Kai kissed me, and Michael scowled in the background. "Michael, can you take Rebecca and Ashlyn home?"

"Yeah," he said. "Come on, let's get out of here."

"Um, bye, John," I said, trying to look cheery to cover for Michael's rudeness. "We'll be in touch."

"Take care of Rebecca," he said quietly. "I have a feeling we're going to need her sooner than later."

As we walked to the car, I watched Michael striding ahead of us. Goddamnit, that guy had the most amazing body. I flashed back to some of the more vivid dreams I'd had about him, and I felt my face get hot. I glanced over at Rebecca, expecting her to make some sort of sarcastic comment, but she just stared straight ahead as she walked. It freaked me out that she still had no trace of a sense of humor.

Back in the apartment, we found Lili doing yoga in the middle of the living room. The pungent scent of incense wafted through the air, and the sound of bells chimed from the stereo. Rebecca coughed, and Lili turned around.

"Oh hey, you're back," she said. She stood up and went into tree pose, balancing on one foot, tucking her other foot up on her opposite thigh and stretching her arms toward the ceiling.

"Yeah, we're going to get dinner. Do you want to join us?" I asked after a moment of hesitation. Lili kind of freaked me out, but I remembered how Rebecca and I had made so little effort with our last roommate, and I felt like I should get to know Lili better.

"No thanks, I'm going out." She dropped her foot to the floor, swooped her arms up as she took a deep breath, and then bent over, put her hands on the ground, and jumped back into downward dog position. Her pants slipped down slightly, exposing the T of black thong underwear riding up above her waistband.

"On a date?" I ventured. "With Jason?"

She took a deep exhale and stood in a forward bend, her head to her ankles, her arms wrapped around the backs of her legs. "On a date, yes, but not with Jason. His name is Matt, and we're going to dinner and then a lecture."

"What's it on?" Rebecca asked, showing the first spark of interest I'd seen in recent memory.

"Tantric sex. Matt and I want to deepen our practice."

Rebecca's face fell, and I steered her toward our room. "Well, we'd better get ready to eat. By the way, do you want to clean tomorrow? The apartment doesn't seem to need it, but we usually get together once a week and clean the whole place."

Lili laughed. "No, I don't clean. That's what the housekeeper is for."

"Housekeeper?" Rebecca and I looked at each other in confusion. "But we don't have a housekeeper."

"Sure we do. Her name is Fiona. She's been cleaning for me for the last couple of years. Don't worry, I've got it covered," she added. "My parents pay for it. She's coming every Thursday afternoon."

"Oh. Well, um, okay, thanks, Lili," I stammered. I felt my face getting hot again, and I pulled Rebecca into our room and shut the door.

"She's a strange person," Rebecca said as she wandered over to her desk. She picked up her stapler absent-mindedly and then put it down again.

"You're okay with having her cleaning lady come into our place?" I asked.

"Sure," Rebecca replied. She looked at me quizzically.

"I guess I'm okay with it, too, then. It just, I don't know, makes me feel a little strange. I've never had one before."

"Really?" I suddenly felt a distance between us, and she looked up at me, startled. "I'm sorry," she said. "I didn't mean to sound so surprised."

"It's nothing," I lied. Just because she'd grown up with servants and penthouses and rich grandmothers and private schools and lived in the coolest city on the planet didn't make her any better than me.

"You know, San Francisco is an amazing city," she said softly as she pulled on a sweater. "Can we go visit your family and just hang out for a weekend?"

We were interrupted by the sound of my phone ringing. I saw Laurel's number and glanced up at Rebecca.

"It's okay," she said. "Go ahead and take it. I can wait a few minutes to eat."

She went into the bathroom, and I sat on my bed and put my phone to my ear. "Laurel, how's it going?"

"Not good. Not good at all. I have to talk to you. Can I come over?" she sounded panicked, and I heard the roar of the freeway in the background.

"Of course! But tell me what happened."

"I can't, I'm driving. I'll be there in a few minutes."

The phone clicked and the call ended. Rebecca poked her head out of the bathroom and looked at me. "No dinner, then?"

I sighed. "I'll meet up with you later, okay?"

She took a coat out of her closet and pulled it on. "Don't worry about me, Ashlyn. I'm going to be fine. Really," she insisted. "Laurel needs you right now more than I do." She gave me a quick hug and left the room.

Ten minutes later, there was a rapid knock on the front door. I quickly opened it, and Laurel strode in. "In here," she said, making a beeline for my room. I chased after her and closed the door behind us.

"Laurel, what in the hell is going on? Are you okay?"

She flopped down on my bed and put her face in her hands. "I'm a complete moron," she said. "Promise you won't judge me."

"Of course not!" I sat next to her and put my arm around her. "But for God's sake tell me what happened."

"I had sex with Jason," she said through gritted teeth. "I don't know how it happened. I went over to his place to pick up a box of pictures he'd accidentally taken. Some of his photos were mixed in, so as we were sorting through them, we started talking about old times. Our time in Japan, some of the crazy stuff that happened when we lived in Isla Vista our first year together, how we first met. And then before I knew it, we were naked in his bed."

I let out a low whistle. "Well, I think that kind of thing can happen to anyone, right? I mean, you were feeling nostalgic, so you had a fling for old time's sake. I mean, even though he's a pig, you don't just stop loving someone just like that."

She shook her head. "I feel like such a slut. I wasn't doing it out of love so much as out of spite. As if to say I can still have him if I want him."

"Do you want him?"

"No! But I want him to want me anyway. And I wanted to get back at your roommate for sleeping with him. I wanted to make her jealous."

I couldn't help laughing out loud. "I'm sorry to tell you this, but she's not exactly the jealous type."

"Maybe not, but I left my panties under the bed just in case."

I stared at her in shock. "You did what?"

"Well, I couldn't very well leave my bra. It would have been too obvious. So I just kicked my panties under the bed." She shrugged. "Jason never cleans, so it's a safe bet she'd find them before he will."

I decided there was no point in mentioning that if anything, Lili's housekeeper was the most likely person to discover the panties, but at that thought, I remembered Rebecca.

"When are you heading up to Dad's? Rebecca and I were thinking of coming up to San Francisco for a weekend, and it would be fun if we could stay with you there while he's away."

"I'm on my way now," she said. "I have to get out of here before I do anything else I'll regret. But yes, come on up next weekend. By then I should be sick of the solitude and will want company." She stood up. "So you don't think I'm a slut?"

"No, but if you need anything else from Jason's, let me go over there instead. I feel confident I can control myself around him."

Laurel punched me on the arm, then gave me a hug and left. As I closed the door behind her, I got a terrible feeling of foreboding, and then suddenly the room whirled around. I sat down heavily on the floor as the room spun and blood pounded in my ears. I closed my eyes and shook my head, trying to get it straight again. A moment later, I opened my eyes and everything had calmed down once more. What in the hell was going on? Just then, I heard Rebecca come back into the apartment, and I got carefully to my feet.

"Here, I brought you dinner," Rebecca said as she entered the room. She handed me a cardboard container, and I opened it to find three slices of veggie pizza. Suddenly, I was starving.

"You're a lifesaver," I said, sitting down and biting into the cheese. "I think my blood sugar was just dropping dangerously low."

She sat on her bed and hugged her knees to her, watching me eat. "Do you think Kai will really be able to talk to some of the neighbors?" she asked.

"Sure," I said. "He's smart, he'll figure out a way to get the information. And in the meantime, since my main job is to get you feeling better again, how would you like to go to San Francisco next weekend and stay at my Dad's place? He's out of town, and Laurel is on her way up there now. We can sit under the redwood trees, watch the boats on the bay. You'll love it."

"That sounds nice," she said. "And can we visit your mom?"

"Absolutely. I'm warning you, she'll want to feed you enough to make you explode, but she's also a very good person to be around when you're feeling crappy."

"I'd like that." Rebecca twirled a piece of hair around her finger in such a familiar way that I felt tears prick the corners of my eyes. I hadn't known until that moment how much I missed my best friend and how desperately I wanted her to be herself again.

## Chapter Twelve: Ghosts

"Ashlyn, I'm just not sure that's a good idea." My father's voice was flat and guarded.

"What do you mean? We're just going to come up for the weekend." I felt my blood pressure rising as I listened to the silence on the other end of the line.

"Your sister is already watching the house," he said at last. "I'd just feel more comfortable if there weren't a lot of people there."

"I'm not a lot of people. I'm your daughter."

"I know that. And I also know that you have a history of making some very poor choices."

"Dad, that was a long time ago! I can't believe you're still holding that against me."

"Let me put it this way: if one of your friends had drunk all your good wine and then stolen your car and crashed it into a tree, I think you'd be concerned about having them stay at your place, too."

"I don't drink anymore," I said, trying desperately to keep my anger in check. "And I have my own car, which I bought with my own money. I've been living on my own for years now and have proven that I'm responsible. Jesus, Dad, it's not like I'm going to burn your house down."

I heard him cover the phone and have a short, muffled discussion with my step-mother. A moment later, his voice came through clearly again. "Alright. You can stay there as long as you stay out of our bedroom and replace any food you eat. I'll be checking in with Laurel every couple of days."

"Thanks, Dad. Your trust in me is inspiring. Have a great time in the Bahamas." I jabbed at my phone to end the call and then threw it across the room. Rebecca stepped tentatively out of the bathroom wrapped in a thick, white towel. She glanced at me, then pushed her wet hair behind her ear as she bent over and picked up the phone where it lay on the floor.

"Conversation with your dad didn't go so well, I take it." She handed me the phone and looked at me with concern.

"You could say that. He still treats me like a drunk teenager. I can't believe the last few years haven't done a thing to change his opinion of me. Sometimes I wonder if *he's* Deimos."

"Don't be ridiculous. He's just afraid. The more opportunities you give him to see the new and improved Ashlyn, the more he'll relax. How often do you call him?"

My conscience gnawed at me. "Not very often. Our conversations are always so tense, I tend to avoid calling him unless I have to."

"That might be a good place to start. Parents don't like to feel like their kids are only interested in talking to them when they need something. If you want him to treat you like an equal, you have to start acting like one."

"Yeah, well, he doesn't call me, either. The phone works both ways."

"But he's not the one who's trying to regain your trust," she pointed out. "If you want this relationship to be different, the ball's in your court." She returned to the bathroom, and a moment later the high-pitched whine of the blow dryer filled the air.

I checked my phone to make sure it was still working. Kai's picture gazed serenely back at me, and I felt myself calm down. Rebecca was right, of course. I had to reach out to my dad more often if I wanted him to see who I really was now and not just keep remembering the stupid train wreck I had been.

Kai's picture suddenly moved. I stared in disbelief as his eyes narrowed and he shook his head disapprovingly. The sound of the blow dryer now sounded like screams. I dropped my phone and covered my ears, and a moment later, there was silence.

I opened my eyes to see Rebecca staring at me. "What's going on? I felt all kinds of fear and panic coming from you."

Breathing hard, I glanced down at my phone. Kai's picture was back to normal. "I don't really know. I just . . . wait a second, did you say you felt my feelings?"

She gaped at me for a second, then covered her mouth. "I did."

I jumped to my feet. "Here, try this." I scratched my arm and held it out to her. Slowly, she reached out and covered the scratch with her hand. I smiled as I felt her healing energy pour into me, and the sting from the scratches immediately faded. She pulled her hand back and looked at me in surprise.

"My powers have returned."

I smiled. "Welcome back, Rebecca. I've really missed you."

She looked down at her hands. "I don't feel any different. Well, I guess I'm not quite as despondent as before. But my heart is still aching like it's never going to heal. What do you think brought my powers back?"

"Maybe you finally healed yourself. Or maybe the need for them is becoming stronger. My guess is that being back here did the trick."

She nodded. "You could be right. Maybe I should stick around here this weekend instead of going up to your dad's. I should get some extra training time in with John. And catch up on my studies."

I felt a twinge of disappointment, but I knew she was right. "Makes sense to me. I can prove my responsibility to my dad another time."

"Oh no, I think you should still go. I'm okay. Really," she said when she saw my skeptical expression. "Something's shifted. I need to get back into my routine so I can move forward. Whatever that looks like." Her face clouded, and I grabbed my phone again.

"Let's check in with Kai and see what he and Michael found out last night, okay?"

A few minutes later, Kai and Michael were sitting in our room. It felt weird for the four of us to be together without Christoph, like a table with a leg missing. The look on Rebecca's face told me that she was noticing the same thing.

"They live in a town called Weinheim," Michael explained. "It's in the southwest of Germany."

"Michael tracked down their address, which is a few doors down from a coffee shop," Kai added. "So I called there to find out whether someone matching Christoph's description was ever in there. Turns out he goes there pretty regularly. They even told me what kind of coffee he drinks."

Rebecca frowned. "They gave a complete stranger all those details about one of their regulars?"

"I think the lady I talked to was just excited to practice her English. We talked for nearly ten minutes. She told me all about the town, too."

I drummed my fingers on my knee. "So okay, great, we know what kind of coffee he drinks, but now what do we do?"

"We send him a letter at the coffee shop. Even though we have his parent's address, you never know whether they're keeping his mail from him or something."

Rebecca looked alarmed. "Why would they do that?"

"Who knows?" Michael answered. "This whole thing makes no sense. Anything's possible at this point."

"Shouldn't we just go and get him?" I asked. "What's the point of sending a letter?"

"It's to give him one more chance to contact us on his own," Rebecca explained, looking hard at Kai. "And you're going to use me as bait."

Michael shifted uncomfortably, and Kai's expression went soft. "I wouldn't call it bait. We're just going to tell him how much he's needed here, how the mission is in jeopardy if he doesn't come back. And if we explain what a hard time you're having, we're hoping it will be enough to make him put aside whatever is going on."

Rebecca got to her feet. "It wasn't enough to keep him from leaving in the first place. But do whatever you think will work." She left the room and closed the door behind her.

"I better go after her." I stood up, and suddenly the room spun around. I swayed for a moment before crumpling to the floor.

"Ashlyn!" Kai and Michael said at the same time. I blinked a few times and looked up. My head was cradled in Michael's arms. Damn, I thought, I will never get used to how fast that guy can move.

"Are you okay?" Kai asked as I slowly sat up.

"Yeah, I just stood up too fast." I glanced at Michael. "Thanks for catching me."

"You sure you're alright?" Michael asked.

Before I could answer, my phone rang. "It's Laurel, excuse me a sec."

"Ashlyn, are you on your way?" she asked. Her voice sounded shaky.

"No, not yet. We were going to leave tomorrow."

"Is there any way you can come sooner? I'm kind of freaking out. I don't think spending time alone was such a great idea, and Mom is working late."

"Oh crap, I'm so sorry. We'll get on the road as soon as we can, okay?"

When I hung up, Kai helped me to my feet. "We shouldn't go up there. I think you're fighting a cold or something."

"No, I'm fine. She really needs us, and I don't think she's in any shape to drive right now."

Michael scowled. "That makes two of you."

Kai stared at me. "If you insist on us going, I'm driving the whole way. I want you to sleep."

I swallowed hard as a gripping sensation caught the back of my throat. Kai was right; I definitely wasn't feeling all that great. But I'd been so focused on Rebecca that I hadn't really paid much attention to it. A weekend away to relax and catch up on sleep was going to be exactly what I needed.

The next morning, we hit the road early, stopping to get gas and sandwiches for the drive up. I immediately felt better as we got on the freeway. So much of my relationship with Kai had been on road trips. It felt like coming home to watch the asphalt disappear under the car as we sped north.

"Kai, what do you think really happened to Christoph?" I asked.

"What do you mean?"

"Do you think he freaked out about Rebecca? Or school? Or suddenly realized he was making his life in the states

109

when he really feels he belongs in Germany? I'm just wondering if you have any theories."

"No," Kai said. "What he's done to Rebecca is inexcusable, especially after what she went through when he was trapped in the snow. Christoph would never willingly hurt her like that, so I can only conclude that he's either there against his will or he's flipped out."

"Do you think that's possible? That the stress of what he went through along with losing a grandfather he was really close to . . . do you think that would be enough to do it?"

"I just don't know. Christoph is very strong physically, but we don't really have any idea how strong he is mentally. We know that he's pretty sensitive."

"True." I watched the trees swaying in the wind and wondered what it must be like to "lose it." My grandmother had suffered from mental illness for many years until they finally figured out the right medication to put her on, and it always scared the hell out of me when we went to visit her in the mental ward. The patients all seemed so unhappy, with their wandering stares, hand wringing, and unintelligible muttering. I didn't know how the nurses and doctors dealt with it day in and day out. It was a living hell, both for the patients and the people trying to help them. I closed my eyes and tried to push the images away. I drifted off to sleep and dreamed of the trees trying to get my attention, waving their branches at me, reminding me of those horrible memories from my past.

When we finally drove into Marin, I had slept for hours but was completely exhausted. I was definitely fighting something, but I had to pull it together for Laurel. I checked my makeup in the mirror as we pulled up in front of my Dad's place, and I was horrified by my reflection. I looked like I'd aged five years.

110

We grabbed our bags and headed into the house. The house looked as it always did, with the white walls, hardwood floors, and sweeping views of the bay dotted with sailboats that looked like toys. We found Laurel sitting on the deck.

"Hey, Laurel," I said. "We're here."

She didn't answer at first. Her eyes were closed, and she was breathing in through her nose and out through her mouth. Finally she opened her eyes and blinked at us.

"Sorry, I was just meditating."

"You meditate?" I asked. "We do that in our martial arts training."

"Something I picked up in Japan," she said as she got up and stretched. "It calms me down when I'm going through a bad patch." She reached out and put her arms around me and then hugged Kai. "I'm really glad you guys are here. I'm kind of a wreck."

"I can imagine." I stroked her hair. "I'm so sorry about all of this."

"Yeah, well, it's my own fault. I knew Jason wasn't happy, but I just ignored it."

"Laurel, it's not your fault he cheated on you," Kai said firmly. "If he wasn't happy, he should have had the balls to tell you and end the relationship. Going and sleeping with someone else was a shitty way to get out of it."

She laughed softly. "He said he didn't realize he was unhappy until he met Lili."

"That's bullshit," Kai insisted. "He knew what he was doing. He just saw something that seemed better at the time and went for it. He'll realize his mistake eventually."

I slipped my arm around Kai's waist. "Not all men are assholes, Laurel. Jason's just being an idiot. If you want him back, I suspect he'll be knocking on your door soon enough."

111

At that moment, I heard a knock at the door. "Weird, I wonder who that could be?" I crossed the living room and opened the front door. Nobody was there.

"Huh," I mused as I looked up and down the street. "Where did they go so fast?" I looked at the door handle, expecting to see a flyer for Chinese takeout or a handyman service, but there was nothing there.

"Where did who go so fast?" Laurel asked.

"Whoever knocked at the door," I replied. "Didn't you hear it?"

Laurel shook her head and looked at Kai, who also looked confused. "I didn't hear anything," he said.

"Oh, well, you probably just didn't hear it out on the deck." I glanced up the street again, suddenly aware that a strange sense of foreboding was crawling up my spine.

Could it be?

Deimos?

Kai reached across me and gently pulled the door closed. "I don't think it's him," he whispered. "C'mon, let's make dinner."

"Oooh, are you cooking?" Laurel asked.

"Yes," I said, slightly distracted. "One of his stir fries, I believe." I took a step into the hallway and suddenly found myself on the ground. The world was spinning around as a faint, metallic whomp whomp whomp sound filled my ears. A moment later, I felt myself being lifted by strong arms.

"What the hell just happened?" Laurel asked in alarm.

"She's fighting a cold," Kai explained. "I think we should put her to bed for a few hours."

He carried me up the stairs to the guest room where we were going to stay. I didn't know why, but staying in the "guest" room always made the hair on the back of my neck stand on end. "Guest" sounded too much like "ghost," and considering how invisible I seemed to be to my dad, it was hard to stay in the ghost room in his house, apparently sealing my fate to being nothing more than a wisp of smoke to him . . . two-dimensional, transparent, and a burden from the past. As Kai tucked me into the soft sheets, I pulled the comforter over my head, trying to drown out the chorus of voices telling me that I'd always just be the second daughter.

## Chapter Thirteen: Delusion

I woke up feeling really weird, like I hadn't slept at all. I sat up and then fell right back down onto my pillow. My head was whirling around. What the hell was wrong with me? I sat up more slowly and looked around. Something wasn't right. Everything seemed . . . what was the word?

I got up and went into the kitchen. The clock said it was two. I stared at it, trying to figure it out. How could it be two o'clock? I pulled back the curtains and looked outside. The sky was cloudy, and from the droplets on the glass, it looked like it had been raining. I couldn't tell if it was early morning or the afternoon. Maybe I was still asleep? If I was dreaming, Deimos would no doubt be making an appearance right about now.

I stood still, listening, but it was silent in the house. Only the gentle creaking of the wood. The sides of the boat, making their way through the waves. Wait, who was at the helm?

I shook my head. What the . . . ?

Food, I thought. I needed to eat. I had somehow slept in until two in the afternoon, and I was having a blood-sugar crash so extreme that I was hallucinating about boats. I filled a pot with hot water and sat watching it until it boiled. I had always wanted to do that. They say a watched pot never boils, but damn it, I was going to prove them wrong.

The water had been boiling for a while before I remembered what I was doing. I put the noodles in the water and set the timer. I watched them boil for a while, and then took a chair by the large windows that looked out over the bay. Where were all those people going on those boats? Were they sailing to other countries? I couldn't imagine what it would be like to sail across the ocean, out of site of land, even out of site of seagulls. Only the sound of the wind, the waves, and the creaking of the boat. Threatening to come apart at the seams.

There was a terrible beeping sound. Was it a fire alarm? How could a fire have started? I'm sailing, not running the engine. The beeping is getting louder. Where is it coming from?

Suddenly, my awareness snapped back into focus, and I realized I was hearing the timer on the stove. My pasta was done. I could eat now. That would put a stop to all this weirdness. When was the last time I went sailing anyway?

Feeling a little woozy, I walked carefully to the stove, turned off the timer and the heat, and grabbed two pot holders. I took the pot over to the sink and poured it out, the noodles now floating calmly, just like tangled seaweed in a foamy sea. I watched as they fell into the sink, clumped into a pile, some of them sliding down the drain with the water. I could almost hear them laughing as they slipped away, like the drain was just the beginning of the world's coolest water slide.

But something was wrong. I stared at the clump of noodles. I couldn't figure it out. I'd forgotten something important, that much I knew. But I just stood there, frozen, unable to move. It felt really important that I figure this out right now.

"What are you doing?" I heard a sleepy voice say. I looked and saw Kai standing there, rubbing his eyes.

"I'm making pasta," I said sadly. "But something is wrong."

He looked blankly at me and then peered down into the sink. "Why didn't you use a colander?"

\* \* \*

A colander. Colander? That word. It means something, something I know. But . . . what does it mean again? My hands reach into my hair and pull, trying to make my brain start working.

"Are you okay?" I hear Kai ask. "It's two o'clock in the morning."

Morning. How can it be morning if it's dark outside? Wait, wasn't it just light out?

I turn to look at Kai, desperate for something to make sense, but he's gone.

And in his place is Deimos.

But this is no dream. This is real.

"I'm going to kill you now," I hear myself say. "I know that's not supposed to be possible, but I thought I made it perfectly clear that you're not going to take Kai away from me ever again." Ah, here comes the rage. And the fire.

A stream of fire jets out of my hands, and Deimos, that sneaky bastard, ducks and runs. A large, black scorch mark appears on the wall. "Ashlyn! What the hell are you doing!"

"Don't you dare speak my name!" I scream as I shoot another stream of fire. It's a snake now, hissing and spitting at its target, but it misses him again and hits the sofa. I watch as it erupts into a bonfire, the flames dancing and reaching for the ceiling. It reminds me of something, but I can't remember what. "Fire in the hole," I whisper, nodding.

Screaming and shouting . . . I wish they'd shut up, whoever they are. Probably Deimos' minions. But I don't care about them right now. The fire is so beautiful, so cleansing. It's going to take all my sorrow and confusion and fear and insecurity and pain and burn it all away. If only the fire would reach the ceiling. It's trying so hard.

"I'm sorry," a whisper says, and suddenly there's a loud cracking sound, a tremendous pressure in the back of my head and that strange, dusty, faraway smell in my nose —

+ + +

Ashlyn fell to the ground, hard. I dropped the frying pan and ran to her side, checking her pulse. It was slow, but steady. Goddamnit, Laurel was barreling down the stairs. I had less than no time to deal with her.

"Kai, what the hell . . . ?" she shouted. "Holy shit, what happened to Ashlyn?"

"Later! Get the fire extinguisher!"

But she just stood there, coughing as she watched the flames licking at the walls. Tearing myself away from Ashlyn, I ran into the kitchen and found the extinguisher under the sink. Good old Robert. At least his predictability extended to safety equipment.

I pulled the pin as I ran back into the living room, aimed the nozzle at the flames, and let it fly. Laurel had finally come to her senses and was on the phone to 911, yelling instructions at them. After a moment, she dropped her phone and raced toward me. "It's not working," she yelled.

"Yeah, I can see that. We have to get out of here." I tossed the extinguisher aside, and, silently praying that I hadn't fractured her neck when I hit her and wasn't about to make things worse, I hoisted Ashlyn up onto my back and staggered for the front door. The room was filling with thick, black smoke, and Laurel was coughing so hard she sounded like she might not make it. She lunged for the door, pulled it open, and we stumbled out into the night, the sound of wailing sirens filling the air.

\* \* \*

The sound of the gull crying wakes me from my sleep. I am lying on a lounge chair on the deck of a ship. The sun is beating down on me, and I roll over to stare up into the white-hot glare. I am parched. Surrounded by water, but so dry. A wave splashes the side of the ship, spreading a fine mist across my face, and my pores suck in the tiny droplets like hungry ghosts. I sit up and hear nothing but the creaking of the ship, the splashing of the waves, the calling of the seagull. I'll be surprised if there's a captain on this vessel.

I stand and walk toward the bow. As expected, I can't see anyone up on the bridge. I am floating God-knows-where with nobody at the helm. That's fine. I'm the captain now, which is how I like things anyway. I half recall a joke from a long time ago. About a control freak.

Jesse? A flash of caramel-colored eyes, and then he's gone. Nothing but the sea, the almost white sky, and . . . suddenly, there's movement in the water below. Dolphins! A huge pod of them, maybe a hundred or more. They're shooting through the water like slick, grey torpedoes, the wisdom in their eyes visible even from the deck of the ship.

Of course. I was meant to be with you.

I jump over the side and dive, plunging deep into the ocean. The water is surprisingly warm but still feels refreshing after sleeping in the hot sun. The dolphins are making sounds like rusty wheels, like laughter. They circle underneath and then bump up against me, pushing me to the surface. But I don't need to come to the surface. The ocean is a strange blend of air and water, and I know that I don't ever have to surface again. I shoot forward, darting in and out of the pod, racing the dolphins through the crystalline blue, whizzing past sea turtles and schools of small fish. Below us is a coral reef, teeming with life. Colorful fish dart in and out of its rocks, and urchins wave their spines at us as we pass.

Up ahead, the ocean becomes lighter, and streaks of sunlight filter through the water. I realize the water is shallower there, which means one thing: land. I don't feel ready to leave the ocean yet, but I'm so thirsty now. I have to get fresh water. I gesture at my pod and point to where I'm going. They seem to know already. They follow me to the shallows and surf in on the breakers. Show-offs.

I shoot out of the water and land on the soft, white sand. It feels strange, more like flannel than sand, but it feels wonderful on my feet. The beach stretches a short distance and ends abruptly at a thick jungle that seems to suck the light into it. Palm trees and mango trees entwined with creeping vines create a formidable wall that stretches as far as I can see.

I fly up and over the canopy of the jungle, trying to peer down through the dark green and brown foliage, but it's impenetrable. The island appears to be mostly flat with a little rise growing up out of the middle like a tumor. I fly back down to the beach and begin walking along the edge of the jungle, listening for the trickle of water. There are many hidden birds making the strangest noises, babbling to each other in their own primitive languages or emitting little beeps and pings. I wish very much that I could see one. I imagine it would be colorful and exotic. But it could also be dangerous, maybe even carnivorous.

I hurry along, and finally, there's the blessed answer to my search: a stream, barely more than a rivulet, emerges from the jungle like blood from an open wound. I kneel and let the fresh, clear water flow into my hands, and when I finally feel washed clean, I scoop it up to my mouth and drink. It tastes so pure and cool, like melted snow. Again and again, I fill my hands and take glorious swallows of this elixir, never knowing before how intensely satisfying a simple drink of water could be.

But now my thirst is finally slaked, and I'm feeling a longing in my gut, the angry growl of hunger beginning to take hold. Drifting up toward the canopy, I explore the trees at the edge of the jungle and pluck mangoes, dates, and coconuts. Do dates and coconuts really grow in the same climate? Something is prickling at the back of my mind, but I'm too hungry to care. I return to the pillowy sand and feast on the tender flesh of the fruits. When my hunger is a little less acute, I am ready to try to deal with these coconuts. I could try breaking them open on a rock, but the beach is smooth and rock-free, and something is telling me that going exploring in the jungle is a b-a-d idea. The sun is dipping lower in the sky, the brilliant white now turning orange, and as a shiver passes through me, I have an idea.

+ + +

"You say you knocked her out?" Laurel and I were standing in the hall outside Ashlyn's room, where nurses were still working on her. The doctor was staring levelly at me, and I felt Laurel's eyes boring into me. Great, now I had to deal with a cover story for Ashlyn *and* convince them I wasn't a wife beater.

"She went crazy and set the house on fire. I tried to stop her, but she was completely out of control. She's got a black belt and is dangerous enough when she's sane, and I had to decide whether to risk her knocking me out and killing all of us or to knock her out. Believe me, it was the hardest thing I've ever had to do."

"How exactly did she set the fire?" the doctor asked.

"She had a frying pan full of burning oil or something. She threw it at the wall and was watching it go up in flames like it was a magical bonfire or something."

"She'd been acting kind of weird," Laurel said in a small voice. "But I didn't see this coming."

The doctor took off his glasses. "Unfortunately, she's not alone. I'm seeing more and more of this kind of thing."

Laurel looked startled. "You mean, you think she's got that thing that's going around, that's making people crazy?"

"It's looking likely. In fact . . ."

But he was interrupted by a shout from inside Ashlyn's room. I ran in and found her sitting cross-legged, looking around with a vacant, glazed look in her eye that froze my blood. Across the room, the cushion on a chair was smoking and covered with the all-too-familiar fire retardant. A nurse was staring palely at Ashlyn, looking like she'd just seen a ghost.

"Restrain and sedate her, now!" I spun around to see two men striding into the room holding up badges. They wrestled Ashlyn down onto her back while the doctor injected something into her arm. She struggled and then went limp, her eyes looking cold and dead. A nurse moved in and put restraints on her while the doctor turned to the men.

"May I ask . . . "

"No," one of them answered curtly. "She's no longer your patient. We're transferring her immediately."

\* \* \*

I gather bits of driftwood, fallen leaves, and fronds and gather them into a little pile. As I work, a cluster of crabs scuttle around amusingly, as if they're watching what I'm doing. Once I've got a big enough pile, I brush off my hands and turn to the crabs.

"Well. I have no idea if there's enough good or evil around here to make this work, but it's definitely worth a try. Are you good or evil crabs?"

They scuttle more frantically, as if they're frightened by what I've just said, and I laugh.

"Funny. I think we might become friends. I have to check with the dolphins, though. I think they're still here." I gaze out into the surf, but they're nowhere to be seen. I'm disappointed, but they'll be back. They probably headed for their sleeping grounds for the night. "Anyway, see what you think of this, crabs!"

I start gathering the fire in my core, building it slowly within me, sweat beading on my brow. I can feel it beginning to take shape, and I stretch out my hands to direct it to the pile, when suddenly the crabs begin shrieking and all charge at me. Several of them grab me by my wrists and ankles with their hard pinchers, and one crab scuttles up my arm and gives me a good, sharp pinch on the inside of my elbow. I feel dizzy, and I sit down, hard.

"Little bastard knows pressure points . . . " I start to say, but then night falls so suddenly that—

+ + +

"Do you think we got away with it?"

John glanced back at me, then went back to driving. "With everyone but Laurel."

I squeezed Ashlyn's hand as the lights from oncoming traffic strobed through the windshield and bounced around the back of the van. I wanted so much for her to wake up, to come back to me. And yet her waking was what I feared more than anything else.

My phone pinged, and I quickly set it on silent mode. I couldn't deal with that situation right now.

* * *

I awaken in a beach hut. The floor is surprisingly hard and cold, and I see that it's made of steel. I hate the way it feels on my skin, and I stand up tentatively. I seem to remember something about dolphins. I want to be with them again—I want to swim and be free—but I don't know where they are. My head is aching, and I look around the hut. It has dark, red walls made of a thick wood that is as hard and cold as the steel floor. In the corner is a metal table and two chairs. The ceiling is so low that I keep thinking I'm going to bump my head as I walk.

On one side of the room is a door painted a rich blue. I try the handle, but it doesn't move. I walk to another door, and this one leads to the outside. I step out onto the sand, which feels chilly in the early morning cold. I'm surprised by a little Siamese cat that comes and rubs against my ankles.

"Hi, kitty. Where did you come from?"

The cat looks at me and starts singing softly. I recognize the tune but can't quite place it. The cat scampers along the sand and I follow, wondering whether it has anyone to feed it.

Maybe it lives off rats and bugs or whatever it can catch. We approach an old, light-blue Volkswagon van, and I see that the side door is open. I peek inside, and to my surprise, I see Laurel sleeping. She looks so peaceful. Laurel . . . how long has it been since I saw her? My brain prickles again, but I can't remember.

The cat jumps inside the van, still singing softly.

"Kitty, let's go," I whisper. "Let's not wake her, okay?"

I pick up the cat and carry her back toward the hut, stroking her tan fur. She begins to sing right in my ear this time, and I remember the tune. It's usually a cheerful, bouncy song, something you would dance to, but she sings it slowly and mournfully. It makes me feel a little sad, and somewhat afraid.

> Oh, where does the sun go
> When the moon hangs low
> In the autumn sky?
>
> It goes to find my love
> The one I've dreamed of
> Since the dawn of time.
>
> Hey, now, hey, now
> Come back now, sun.
> Hey, now, hey, now
> And make us one.

As we approach the hut, I see a man step out of the doorway. I'm so surprised that I drop the cat, who is quiet now. The man is dressed in a white linen shirt and khaki pants that are rolled up above his ankles. He's holding a string of several small fish, and the cat immediately starts purring and circling his feet.

"Do you live here?" I ask.

"Sometimes. Would you like to join me for breakfast?"

"Do you have something other than fish?"

He smiles. "Follow me." We walk into the hut, which is now noticeably cooler than the outside. He sets the fish down on the table, then lifts the lid on a small chest and pulls out a basket of fruit. He holds it out to me, and I choose a bright yellow banana. I pull back the peel and, suddenly ravenous, eat the fruit in three bites. He tosses the smallest fish to the cat, who pounces on it and begins shaking it in her mouth as if to ensure that the fish is truly dead. I drink from a coconut he offers me, savoring the coolness as it quenches my thirst. I hand it back to him, and he takes a long drink.

"Do you know Laurel?" I ask.

"Is she the girl in the van?"

"Yes. She's my sister."

He frowns. "There have been a lot of people camping around here lately, and several of them have disappeared. You should tell your sister to clear out while she still can."

"Disappeared? What do you mean?" I ask in alarm.

But before I can answer, the front door suddenly slams shut, and the room becomes pitch black. The cat begins singing the song again, only this time with an eerie, foreboding tone. Hearing this cheerful song sung like a warning makes my skin crawl. Behind me, I hear the other door open, and something crawls across the floor. Before I can move, I feel bony fingers on my face and hear sniffing at my neck. I try to scream, but no sound comes out. The cat sings louder as my heart pounds. Through it all, I hear the sound of the man's calm breathing, which suddenly infuriates me to the breaking point.

A fireball bursts from my hand and hovers there, illuminating the room, and I recoil in terror. Before me is an old woman with long, tangled white hair and a feral look in her eye. An evil sneer plays on her lips.

"This is no camper," she screeches in a voice like breaking glass.

"No," the man says quietly. "There will be others, mother."

"The last one left a bitter taste in my mouth. Dirty kids. Ruining our jungle. Their flesh tastes like wine and tobacco."

I feel vomit rising in my throat. I shoot into the air and blast toward the door, but it's sealed and I bounce right off it. Stunned, I try again, but I can't break it open. I hurl a fireball at it, then at the walls, anything to get out of this horrible cage. But I'm trapped. I hover in the far corner of the ceiling, and the woman lets out a terrible laugh.

"Oh, don't like our company, is that right? The pot calling the kettle black, you stupid tramp. Who do you think you are?"

"I know I'm not one of you, and that's enough," I manage to sputter. I'm shaking uncontrollably now, terrified of falling to the floor, even though I'm already within the man's reach. But he sits quietly.

"Not one of us!" she howls. "No, you're not. You're far, far worse than that. You harm everyone who loves you. You cause evil to spread while you think you're doing good. You are *evil that cannot be destroyed.*"

My head starts to spin. A voice inside my head tells me not to listen to this banshee, that she is trying to break me. But another voice, a voice of doubt, creeps in.

"That's right!" she screams. "Why do you think you of all people became an Alchemist? What have you done that's restored the balance of evil? Everything you do just makes it worse. Because you're not fighting Deimos . . . you *are* Deimos!"

She shrieks her maniacal laugh, and I hurl a fireball at her. She becomes engulfed in flames, and I send fireball after fireball at her, but she just laughs and dances wildly, the fire not harming her in the slightest. "You can't kill evil! So you can't kill yourself!"

"I am not you! And I am not Deimos, you evil psychopathic cannibalistic harpie!" I am determined not to succumb, and if hurling Jesse-style insults at her is . . . is . . .

Jesse. Rebecca. *Kai.*

"Kai, help me!" I scream. "Wherever you are, I need you right now!"

"Help me!" she taunts, but her voice has lost some of its strength, and I notice her gaze is starting to dart around the room.

"Michael, Christoph! Help Laurel! Get her out of here and make sure she's safe!"

"She is safe," the man says, still sitting calmly. The woman turns on him and lets out a piercing shriek, but he doesn't seem to notice.

"Rebecca, please, *please*," I begin to sob. "I need you. Please help me."

At that moment, a hole appears in the ceiling of the hut, and a blinding shaft of light bursts through, illuminating the hideous old woman. I plug my ears against her screams as she begins to disintegrate before our eyes, twisting and writhing, fighting it with surprising strength, but she is no match for the light. She finally dissolves into nothing but tiny particles that melt like snowflakes and are gone.

\* \* \*

127

The scene changed as if a scrim had been lifted on a stage. Instead of a hut, I was in a small steel shed. In the spot where the man had been, a person dressed in a fire-proof suit was sitting perfectly still on the floor. In the dim light, I couldn't make out his face through the mask. But I knew that posture anywhere.

"John? Is that you?" I asked timidly.

"Yes, Ashlyn. We're all here. The others are outside."

I blinked and looked around. It was dim and dusty in the shed, with only the light from one small window covered with bars. I flew over and looked outside, and sure enough, there was Kai, Rebecca, and Michael. I rapped on the glass, and they all took a step back, looking fearful.

"What's going on? Where am I? Why are they outside?" I drifted down to the floor. "And why are you in a fireproof suit?"

John stood up slowly. He carefully pulled off his hood and looked deeply into my eyes. He looked as if he hadn't slept in days, and there were far more lines around his eyes than I'd ever noticed before. "Do you know where you are?"

I looked around again. "In some kind of steel shed, it looks like. But I can't remember how I got here. I have been having the weirdest dreams, the most horrible nightmare ever." I saw the look of concern start to soften a bit. "John, what happened to me?"

Slowly, carefully, he took a step forward and put his arms around me, holding me in a long embrace. Now I was really worried, but it felt nice to be held. It seemed like it had been a really long time.

At that moment, I heard the sound of my mother's voice. I took a step back. "John, I think I'm starting to hallucinate again."

He looked concerned. "What are you seeing?"

"It's what I'm hearing . . . it sounds like my mom." I peered over his shoulder at the only door. It seemed like my mom's voice was getting closer.

". . . and I'm not staying out here any longer, damn it. Let me in!" Just then, the door flew open, and my mom burst in.

"Oh, Ashlyn!" she cried. "I was so worried about you!" She practically shoved John out of the way and threw her arms around me, squeezing me so tightly I gasped.

"Mom, is that really you?"

"Of course it is. John, have you explained everything to her?"

I looked at John, who had the strangest look on his face I'd ever seen. "No, Elise, she only just came back to us. I don't know how long we have. This might just be temporary."

My mom laughed, making me feel even crazier than I had when I'd been hallucinating. "John, you underestimate Rebecca."

I felt light-headed, and a moment later I was sitting on the ground. Mom and John rushed to my side. I searched my mom's piercing blue eyes.

"Mom, what . . . what do you mean? About Rebecca?" The world was beginning to spin slightly.

"I mean she's one of the most powerful Empaths I've ever met."

A moment later, everything went black.

## Chapter Fourteen: The Empath

"Sorry, sweetie, I should have broken it to you more gently."

I was lying on the floor, my head in my mom's lap. She was stroking my hair. Kai was sitting next to us, looking like he was longing to hold me, but my mom had her arm firmly around me. Now seemed like a weird time for the protective mother-bear routine, but I was too confused to argue. Rebecca, Michael, and John sat around us, watching. The looks on their faces were actually pretty comical.

"I don't care how you break it to me, Mom, just explain what the hell you're talking about. How do you know about Empaths?"

"Ashlyn, for heaven's sake, do you honestly think you're the only Soterian in the family?"

I sat up. "Wait, are you saying . . . ?"

"Of course I am. Jesus, honey, how long have you had your powers and it took you this long to figure it out?" She laughed. "You honestly think I joined the Peace Corps? On purpose?"

"You weren't in the Peace Corps?" I asked weakly.

"Of course not! What, you thought I underwent a complete personality transplant at some point? I've always hated traveling. And why do you think I was always so protective of you and Laurel?"

I gasped. "Is she a Soterian, too?"

"No, thank God. She managed to dodge it. I was hopeful when your powers didn't show up by your twentieth birthday that you were in the clear, too. But you always did attract trouble. I suppose it was meant to be." Her mouth was pressed into a hard line. I still couldn't wrap my brain around what she was saying. How could she be a Soterian? How could she know about all this?

"What kind of Soterian were you?" I asked. She smirked at me, and I laughed. "An Empath. Of course. You've always seemed to know what I was feeling. Although," I turned to look at John. "I thought once you've restored the balance, your powers fade for good."

"They fade, but they're not completely gone," Mom explained. "Your natural gifts are enhanced. I suppose you'll be hooked on triathlons more than ever after this."

"Mom, I'm sitting on the floor of a steel shed, having just come back from the depths of insanity, and you're worried about me doing *triathlons*?"

"Fair enough." She stood and dusted herself off. "Anyway, you're going to have to have a long talk with your dad. He's losing his mind."

"Does he know about this?" I asked in horror.

"Yes, I explained it all to him and to Laurel. She was ready to beat back those men with a stick when they wanted to take you from the hospital, so I had no choice. Now I think she's just furious that you didn't tell her. Your father already knows about the Soterians, of course. It was the cause of many a fight between us, believe me. He was terrified that something was going to happen to me, and he was always worried that you kids would end up with powers, too."

I looked down, trying to imagine what my dad must have gone through. He was such a strong, powerful man. But he couldn't do a thing about the evils we had to fight. It must have made him feel so helpless. And my dad didn't do helpless very well.

"I'm sorry," I said. "I hate that I've made you guys worry."

"Yes, well, I think he's more concerned about his house right now."

"His house?"

Kai cleared his throat. "Do you remember what happened at his place?"

I thought back, to just before the weird dreams started. I remembered being at his house, but that was about it.

"Not really. I was dreaming about crabs and all kinds of weird stuff. But I don't remember what happened before all that."

Kai looked pained. "You, um, you threw a fireball at me. It's okay, I ducked," he said quickly as I gasped. "But unfortunately, it hit that tapestry on the wall, which went up in flames."

"That and the sofa," my mom added.

I felt the sickening horror building in my stomach. "No. You are not telling me that I burned down my father's house. Please tell me that's not what you're saying."

"Define *burned down*," Michael said.

"Oh shit, oh shit, oh shit!" I jumped to my feet and started pacing, ignoring the looks of alarm on everyone's face. "He's going to kill me! I promised I was going to take such good care of his place, that he needed to trust me! And now this!"

"Honey, it's fine, he understands," Mom said. "His insurance is paying for it. Evelyn is delighted that she's finally going to get to paint those hospital-white walls she never liked and is already picking out the colors."

I sank back to the floor. "So how did I get here?"

"Theresa hired a couple of men to pose as FBI and get you sedated and out of there," John said. "You were risking exposure every second, not to mention the risk of burning down the hospital. We brought you here, to a fireproof shed, where you couldn't hurt anyone, while Rebecca worked on you around the clock. But it was very difficult. You kept throwing fireballs."

I looked over at Rebecca. "Thank you, Bec. I'm so sorry."

"It's fine," she said in a strained voice. "To be honest, it was nice to have something else to focus on."

"There's still no word from Christoph?" I asked, but the answer was written on all their faces. "Okay, that's it, we've waited long enough. I'm going after him."

"What?!" rang a chorus of voices in disbelief.

"Something isn't right. Think about it: Christoph is one of the most faithful people on the planet. He loves Rebecca, he loves being a Soterian, and he would die for any of us. What's the most upset you've ever seen him before now?"

There was silence for a few moments, and then Rebecca spoke. "Probably after the incident at the Golden Gate Bridge, when he felt like he failed you."

"Exactly. My guess is that something has happened that made him feel like he failed Rebecca, or all of us, in some way. We need to find out what it is so that I can bring him back."

"That's all very nice, but you don't have to be the one to go," my mom insisted. "You've already been through enough. Stop playing the hero."

"Mom, I'm a Scout, and more importantly, I'm an Alchemist. In all probability, Deimos is the only evil strong enough to make Christoph abandon us all, so there's a chance

I'll have to go up against him to get Christoph back. Michael, you know I'm right," I said, turning to him for support. "Back me up."

He looked hard at me and didn't speak for a moment, but finally his eyes softened with a look of resignation. "I don't like it, but yeah, I have to say that you're right."

I turned to Rebecca and Kai. "Take care of each other. I'll be back soon, with a less confused Christoph in tow."

My mom looked furious. "You need to talk to your dad before you go running off to Germany."

"I will. And don't worry, Mom. I'll be really careful. I promise."

Kai stood up. His expression was blank as he took my hand and helped me to my feet. "Let's go. We have a lot of planning to do."

I shaded my eyes as we walked out into the brilliant sunlight. "Tell me again how long I was locked in that shed?"

"Almost a week," Kai answered. Suddenly, he stopped, a faraway look in his eyes.

"What is it?" I asked.

"Just a thought," he said slowly. "I think we should take a blood sample from you and send it to Kenji."

"From me? Why?"

"Kai, that's brilliant," Rebecca said as she and Michael caught up with us.

"You might be onto something there," Michael agreed.

I looked at each of them in turn. "Would someone care to fill me in, please?"

"You've just beat a virus that nobody else has recovered from," Rebecca explained.

"Yes, because you healed me," I pointed out.

"Right, but healing works with your body. Mostly it just speeds up your own natural healing process. So in your case, it probably supercharged your immune system so that it could fight the virus. If we can isolate the antibody that overcame the virus, we might be able to develop a cure."

"Let's stop at the vet clinic," Kai suggested as we all climbed into his car. "I can take the sample and send it to Kenji with no questions asked.

"*You're* going to do it?" Michael asked. "At the vet clinic? She's a person, not a hamster."

"Back off, Michael," I snapped. "We'll avoid a lot of questions this way. But I have one request: let Rebecca do it."

"Me?" she asked in surprise. "Why?"

"Because you've missed a lot of school with this whole episode, and the least I can do is let you practice taking blood from me. Can't be a doctor without being able to draw blood. Kai will show you how to do it."

"Piece of cake," Kai said. Michael looked sulky but kept his mouth shut.

"Does Marlowe know anything about my illness?" I asked him.

"No, I told her you were still in San Francisco."

"You lied to her?" I asked in surprise.

"Didn't really have a choice, did I?"

I was struck again by what a terrible situation Michael was in, not being able to tell Marlowe the truth about us. It didn't make it any easier that I had told Kai about us right from the start, and I knew Michael still resented me for it, even though Kai had become our Keeper as a result. As we pulled onto the freeway, I closed my eyes, still feeling a bit dizzy. As usual, I had no idea how I was going to pull off this next mission, but I had to do everything in my power to help Christoph and bring him home. I peeked out of the corner of my eye at Rebecca, who looked incredibly pale and thin. No, failing at this mission simply wasn't an option.

As we pulled into the parking lot of the vet clinic, Kai suddenly stopped the car.

"What's up?" I asked. He was staring straight ahead, his eyes narrowed.

"I just realized that maybe we should go around back. I'll run in, grab some needles and vials, and we'll do this at home. Too many people on staff right now." He turned the car around and drove around the block. There was a strange mix of emotions emanating from Kai. I glanced back at Rebecca, who just shrugged at me. I was about to question him, but my head suddenly started spinning.

"Ashlyn!" Rebecca said. She put her hands on me, and I felt her soothing healing pouring into me. My head cleared almost immediately.

"You better take it easy," Kai said.

"No kidding," I said, rubbing my throbbing temples. "I definitely do not want a relapse."

By the time we finally got home, I was exhausted. Rebecca propped pillows behind my back so I could relax in a semi-reclining position. Kai tied a rubber tube around my arm and then showed Rebecca how to find a good vein. He was just showing her the best angle for putting in the needle when the bedroom door swung open.

"Ashlyn," Lili said as she strode into the room. "I thought I heard your voice and—" she stopped short and her mouth dropped open.

"Lili," I stammered. "Um, this isn't what it looks like."

Her eyes were flashing with anger, and her chin jutted out as she began talking very fast. "Seriously? Heroin? Are you kidding me? Do you know what that shit does to people? Rebecca, how the hell could you shoot her up?"

Rebecca stepped forward. "It's not heroin. We need to take follow-up blood samples for the next few days to make she's not getting another infection, and they're letting me do it as part of my training. Look, no syringe, just a needle and a Vacutane."

Lili's face softened and she exhaled. "That's a relief. Sorry for busting in here like this, but I've been dying to see you. Rebecca said you were in quarantine because your flu was so contagious, so I couldn't come visit." She walked over and sat next to me on my bed. "You look really pale. Are you sure you're up to being Rebecca's guinea pig?"

I smirked. "Anything for a friend."

She smiled. "I'm glad you guys aren't on smack. I didn't want to think that stuff Kelly is writing is true. You had me worried for a minute there."

"No need to worry, we--wait, what stuff? What do you mean?"

"In her blog." Lili looked at Kai, who was looking down at his feet, and then looked back at me. "You haven't seen her blog yet?"

"No! Kai, do you know anything about this?"

He shrugged. "It's not a big deal. She's just writing some crap. It's nothing to worry about."

Lili glanced around at us and then cleared her throat as she stood up. "Okay, then. I'm heading down to dinner. See you all later." She hastily left the room, and I felt my heart pounding.

"Kai . . ." I warned.

He sat next to me on the bed. "Really, it's not a big deal. She's trying to cash in on the band's popularity by writing crap about me." He hesitated. "About *us*. But it's no big deal. Toby has advised us to ignore it and people won't pay any attention."

I jumped to my feet and grabbed my laptop. "Are you kidding? This kind of thing can totally go viral." I did a quick search for "Kai Anderson" plus "Waterfall" and quickly scanned the results.

Oh. My. God.

## Chapter Fifteen: The Price of Fame

"This is slander!" I shouted. "How can you say we should do nothing?"

I pulled at my hair as I paced around the living room of the The Manor. Kai, Ryan, and Rebecca sat on the couch looking grim, while Toby was standing in the middle of the room trying to talk me down.

"Because anything we do, anything at all, will throw fuel on the flames."

"Not if you come back with the truth about her! About how she's the jealous ex-girlfriend who regrets now more than ever her idiotic decision to leave Kai. She said we're selling heroin, for God's sake! Look at this, look!" I grabbed my laptop and read aloud. "'Kai and Ashlyn have a long history of getting wasted and fighting in public. One night they were so drunk he fell over and crashed through the living room window. Other times they hole up in her room for days with her roommate, Rebecca, doing heroin and throwing sex parties. I had to watch helplessly as they got my friend Tracy, who shared their apartment for a while, hooked on a nasty drug they introduced to the party scene in Santa Barbara. It took her months of rehab to recover.'" I slammed my laptop on the table. "The stupid bitch doesn't even know that addicts on a heroin binge don't do *anything*, let alone throw parties. We have to set the record straight."

Toby approached me and put his hands on my shoulders. "If we print a rebuttal, it starts a flame war. If you guys start doing charity work, it'll look like you're trying to boost your image and it'll seem to confirm what she's saying. If we hire a lawyer, the press will hear about it and it'll be all over the news." His deep blue eyes stared hard into mine. He looked pretty worn out, and I felt a stab of guilt.

I sighed and sat heavily on the arm of the couch next to Kai. "I feel so powerless."

Toby nodded. "It'll pass. And then the next hater will come along. You can't battle them all. This is one of the downsides of being famous."

"We're far from being famous," Ryan scoffed. He rubbed his hands on his jeans and then got to his feet. "I'm going to the pub. I'll catch you guys later."

"Are you coming to practice tonight?" Kai asked.

"Hell, yeah. We gotta smooth out the edges on those tracks before we go back into the studio." Ryan disappeared into the pale light of the late afternoon, and I felt the sudden urge to curl up and take a nap.

"Ashlyn, you should rest," Rebecca suggested. "You only just got back on your feet."

"It sounds like it was a horrible flu," Toby said. "They wouldn't even let me call, said you needed to sleep. I'm glad you're feeling better now."

"But Rebecca's right," Kai broke in. "You need to rest. Try to forget about all this crap with Kelly. People will get bored with her pathetic lies and move on."

I stood up and Kai jumped to his feet to help me. I felt dizzy for a moment and had to lean on him to steady myself. I couldn't believe how weak I still felt. But I could feel the power slowly seeping back into my veins, and if anything, Kelly's latest attempt to undermine us only strengthened me with anger.

"I can't believe she's still saying you dumped her," I said as we made our way back to the apartment.

Rebecca shook her head. "I can't believe she said you were in a gang."

"Technically, she said I was sleeping with a gang, not that I was a member."

We looked at each other and burst out laughing. And in that moment, as the sun dipped down beyond the horizon, and we stood there on the walkway laughing until we cried, I felt like we were just normal college students again, worried about mid-terms and exes and whether you could live better on ramen or chips and salsa. Deimos and the Soterians and burning down my dad's house and Christoph's disappearance and the epidemic all just seemed like visions from a bad dream that we would shake off in the morning.

But a moment later the weight of all of it dropped heavily on my shoulders again. Rebecca looked at me sadly. "One thing at a time, okay?"

"Yeah. First rest, then food." I took a deep breath. "And then, I face my dad."

Later that night, I sat anxiously watching the clock. Kai was at band practice, and Rebecca was at the library studying. My dad's response to my email requesting that we have a video chat at eight o'clock had been just one word: "Okay." That didn't bode well for the conversation, but it had to be done. Mom had encouraged me just to be completely honest and speak from my heart. It was weird that I didn't have to hide anything from them anymore, but somehow that didn't make it any easier. My dad still thought I was an irresponsible moron, Alchemist or no.

I flipped open my laptop, put in my ear buds, and launched the video app. Dad wasn't online yet, and I tapped my fingers nervously watching the icon next to his name. *Breathe*, I thought. *Just breathe*. It's going to be over soon.

Ping. Robert Woods is online.

"Here we go." I took a deep breath and started the video call. It took several agonizing seconds before he answered and his face popped into view. He wasn't smiling.

"Hi, Dad," I said in a squeaky voice. I cleared my throat. "How are you?"

"I've been better," he replied.

"Before we talk about anything else, I just want you to know that I am really, truly sorry. I was completely out of my mind from that horrible virus that's putting people in mental hospitals all over the country, and I had no idea what I was doing. I swear I didn't burn your house down because of carelessness or being drunk or anything like that. I was literally insane."

He stared at me unblinkingly for a few moments. "So, let's get right to it. When were you planning to tell me that you're a Soterian."

"Well, never, actually. I didn't know that was an option."

"Does Kai know?" he asked icily.

"Yes. He's our Keeper."

His eyes softened, and he nodded. "That explains a few things."

"It does?" I asked in surprise.

A hard look crossed his face. "Yes. Your mother had an affair with their Keeper. Oh, I see she neglected to tell you that."

My head started spinning slightly. "We . . . we haven't had a lot of time to talk yet. I just came out of the delirium this morning. But wow, Dad, I had no idea. Was that the real reason you got divorced?"

"It was one reason. The final nail in the coffin." He looked so hurt, even vulnerable for a second, which made me feel slightly sick. "Look, Ashlyn, I can't tell you how to live your life, but this Soterian business is bad news. You run all over the place acting like a superhero risking your neck and making bad decisions, and for what? No lasting good comes from it. There will always be evil; you can't get rid of it."

I sighed. "No, you can't. But that's why we're needed. To keep it in check."

"Yes, yes. Believe me, I've heard all this before. *Ad nauseum*. I didn't understand it then, and I don't understand it now. But you're a lot like you're mother, and you're going to do what you're going to do."

"Actually," I laughed, "I think I'm a lot like you in that way. You're not exactly a follower."

Dad pursed his lips and nodded slowly. "So. What mission are you on now?"

"Right now, it's to make amends with you. How bad is your house?"

"Don't worry about it. Insurance is covering everything."

"I'll pay the deductible, then. How long is it going to take to repair everything?"

He gave me a curious look. "I covered the deductible. But I appreciate the offer. It's going to be a few months, probably longer if Evelyn has anything to do with it. She's all excited to redecorate."

"Might as well give in to the inevitable, Dad."

"In more ways than one, I suppose." He looked hard at me. "Take care of yourself, Ashlyn. I really don't want anything to happen to you."

I swallowed the lump in my throat. "I will, Dad. We have two really great units. Well, our Sentries are out of commission at the moment, but--"

He looked alarmed. "Why?"

"Well, one of them is one hundred percent focused on research, and one of them went back home to Germany. To tell you the truth, I'm planning to go there in a few days to talk him into coming back."

"You're going to Germany?" Dad was silent for a moment. "When are you leaving?"

"I haven't bought my ticket yet, but I'm hoping to go at the end of the week. Why?"

He had a very strange look on his face. "I think I'd like to go with you."

I paused. "Excuse me?"

"I'm overdue for a visit to the house in Gestacht. And I wouldn't mind getting out of here for a week or two while Evelyn does her thing." He glanced around and looked slightly claustrophobic.

"Um, okay, but I'm going to be--"

He waved his hand impatiently. "Yes, I know, on Soterian business. But you've never been to Germany, and you're going to need some help getting around."

I saw a spark in his eye that said that argument was fruitless. Once my dad got an idea in his head, there was no point in trying to talk him out of it. I smiled at him. "Okay, Dad. It'll be great to have you along. I was kind of dreading going by myself."

"I'll get the tickets tonight. You have your passport?"

144

"Yep, all set." I looked down at my hands. I was excited and terrified at the same time. What were we going to talk about for eleven hours on a plane? "Oh, and Dad? Thank you. For everything. I know I wasn't the easiest daughter in the world, and you've always done the best you could."

He shook his head. "I just wish you hadn't had to go down this road."

We ended the call, and I slowly closed my laptop. How amazing that I had started out worrying that Dad was never going to speak to me again, and by the end he was buying my ticket to Germany and accompanying me. I called my mom to tell her about it, but she seemed wholly unsurprised.

"Good for him, I'm glad he's going with you. The worst thing for bystanders is not being able to do anything. This gives him something to do. And I'll feel a lot better knowing he's watching out for you."

I laughed. "Mom, I'm the one who can throw fireballs, remember? But yeah, it'll be nice to have him along, especially since he's fluent in German." I paused, unsure whether to broach the next topic with her.

"What is it, Ashlyn?" Mom asked.

I took a deep breath. "Dad said that you cheated on him with your Keeper."

"He did, did he? Well, I'm sure that's how he remembers it. Technically, your Dad and I had broken up, and Stephano and I—"

"Stephano?"

"Our Keeper, Stephano. He and I fell in love and went out for a few years while your Dad and I were broken up. When I returned from Central America, Stephano stayed behind, and I got back together with your dad."

I was aghast. "You never saw him again?"

145

"Not until many years later. Stephano came to visit. I went out with him, and we stayed out all night talking about old times. Nothing happened between us, but your father was absolutely furious. He claimed I was still in love with him and never forgave me."

"Were you still in love with him?" I asked tentatively.

"Of course. That wasn't going to go away just because I made my life with someone else. But I was also in love with your Dad. He just couldn't understand that I had room in my heart for more than him."

I pondered what Mom had just told me. She'd been in love with this Stephano guy, but went back to my dad. And yet that wasn't enough for him. He had to have her whole heart or nothing. "Why are relationships so damn complicated?" I asked.

"On that subject, what is your strategy for bringing Christoph home?"

I exhaled deeply. "I really don't know, Mom. I'm just going to speak from my heart, I guess. Tell him how miserable Rebecca is, how much we need him."

"My suggestion is to listen more than you talk. Something major is going on with that guy to make him pull a stunt like this. You need to find out what it is before you can talk some sense into him."

"Good point. Listen, Mom, I have to go. I'll call you tomorrow, okay?"

"Sleep well, Ashlyn. I'm glad you're back in the land of the sane."

"That's entirely a matter of opinion," I snorted as I stole a glance at Kelly's latest blog post on my laptop. I was trying very hard not to read them, but it was impossible to resist. The vitriol of that horrible shrew was beyond even my expectations. I wondered if I could ever truly find compassion for someone so bent on making other people miserable.

Later that evening, as I lay on my bed listening to the sounds of the waves a couple blocks away, I heard the sound of Kai's car pull into the parking lot. It gave its signature whine it always made whenever he pulled the wheel hard to the left, and then there was silence. Exhausted from replaying the conversation with my dad over and over while simultaneously trying to plan what I was going to do once I got to Germany, I slowly got up and pulled on my shoes and jacket. I desperately needed to see Kai and just feel loved and centered again.

I walked down the steps to meet him, but he still hadn't come through the complex yet. Probably listening to the end of a song, I thought. But as I stretched to hear him, I heard something else entirely. It sounded like he was talking to someone in an urgent whisper.

Quickening my step, I hurried toward the parking lot and met up with him just as he walked into the courtyard. He was moving quickly, an intense look of concern across his face. His eyes widened in surprise when he saw me.

"Ashlyn! What are you doing out here? Did you talk to your dad?"

"Yeah, I was just coming to tell you about it. Who was that you were talking to in the parking lot?"

Kai shifted his guitar to his other shoulder. "It's nobody. Just . . . just someone who's been reading Kelly's blog."

I felt anger well up inside of me as I turned and glared toward Kelly's apartment. It was dark, as usual. "I've had enough of her crap. I swear, next time she's around, she better hope I'm in a better mood than I am right now."

"Well, fortunately, she never seems to be around anymore. Probably hiding out someplace where she can write her horror stories in peace." He took my hand and we strolled toward The Manor. "Can you come up for a while? I feel like I haven't seen you in months."

"I thought you'd never ask."

He gave me that beautiful half smile that always made me feel so much calmer. "Do you want to tell me about your dad?"

"I did, but now I just want to forget everything and spend some time focusing on you. But just so you're not in suspense, we've made amends. He's even buying my ticket to Germany. And . . . you're not going to believe this . . . he's coming with me."

Kai stopped. "To Germany?"

"Yeah, to Germany. I know, it's totally weird. But actually I'm kind of glad. He speaks German, and he might be helpful. I think it'll be good for him to feel like he's useful and not completely powerless."

I felt a tiny stab of pain coming from Kai, and then my own words hit me. "Oh shit, Kai, don't take that the wrong way."

"It's okay," he said softly. "I guess your dad and I have more in common than I thought. But I'm not completely powerless. I have your love, anyway."

I turned and cupped his face in my hands. The moonlight shone on his hair, and the trees cast shadows across his face. His eyes looked almost blue in the silvery light. "My God," I whispered. "You are so gorgeous, I can hardly stand it."

His gaze held mine, and then he kissed me with his incredibly sweet, warm, soft lips. I melted into his arms, feeling for the first time in as long as I could remember that I was right where I belonged.

A moment later, the night was pierced with the sound of breaking glass coming from the parking lot.

"What the—?" Kai began, but I was already running toward the sound. I heard a car shift into gear and race down the street. I looked around for Kai's car, already knowing what I was going to see.

"ASSHOLE!" was spray-painted on the hood in large, black letters. His windshield was smashed in, and mounds of tiny squares of glass covered his dashboard and front seat. I stood paralyzed for a second, then ducked in between a couple of cars. Just as I was crouching down getting ready to disappear, Kai grabbed my arm.

"Don't," he said. "It's no use."

"What do you mean? Kai, let go of my arm. I'm going to find out who did this!"

"I know who did this." His voice was so calm, so defeated, that it suddenly struck me. He'd been keeping something from me. Again. "Come on, we need to talk."

I followed him without a word to his apartment, breathing hard, trying to steady myself for what was to come. As we climbed the stairs, I thought I saw a light go out in Kelly's apartment. I listened but couldn't hear anything from inside. Well, I wasn't going to give her the satisfaction of blowing up his window this time. Whatever it was, I was going to handle it like an adult.

"Yes," he said without preamble the second he had closed his bedroom door behind us. "I've been keeping something from you. But this time I had an excuse. You were sick." He sat down on the bed and pulled out his phone. I stood warily at a distance. I felt like I'd swallowed a bomb and he was holding the detonator.

"I was planning to tell you tomorrow, because I thought band practice was going to go too late and you'd be asleep, but when I saw you in the courtyard, I decided right then that

I was going to tell you tonight. Even though all I wanted to do was go straight to bed with you and forget everything."

"Kai, you've got five seconds to tell me what's going on." I was amazed at how calm my voice sounded.

He sighed. "I have a stalker. Her name is Debbie. At first I thought she was just a really enthusiastic fan. But lately it's gotten bad." He held up his phone. "Here are the texts she's sent me. I've been keeping them in case something like this happened."

I took his phone and scrolled through the texts. I felt instantly sick. It was so completely obvious from the very beginning what this girl was after. His responses to her were things like "Aw, that's so sweet of you" and "Glad you liked our music," but eventually he became more distant, and finally he stopped responding altogether. The end of the thread was fifteen texts from her with no response from Kai.

I sat heavily on the bed next to him and handed him the phone. "You're a total moron, Kai. I love you so much, but how many times have I told you to look out for this kind of thing? That your being so oblivious to how hot you are was going to get you in trouble one day?"

"I know," he said. "You were right. About me being oblivious, that is. It got kind of hard to ignore when she started showing up in person, though."

"When did that start?"

"Only a couple days ago. She was outside the vet hospital when we went to get the blood draw kit. And tonight she was outside Max's place when I got there, and then she must have followed me home."

My heart skipped a beat. "And what did she say to you in the parking lot?"

"She asked me out. I explained that I wasn't interested, that I was with you, and she started repeating a bunch of the stuff she'd read in Kelly's blog about you. I told her that it was all lies, that Kelly was my ex-girlfriend with an axe to grind, and that I'm in love with you and that we're really happy together. She seemed kind of embarrassed. She even apologized and then said she wished us well. I thought that was it. Guess I really am a moron."

He stood up and walked to the window, staring out into the moonlight. "If only I'd known how to handle it better, this wouldn't have happened. It was just so cool, having a fan." He let the curtain drop. "I just wish she'd actually been into our music, you know?"

I nodded. "Yeah, I know you're not actually interested in being a rock star. You just want to play music and have people like it. But that's not all there is to it, sadly. Once you're in the public eye, all this other shit happens, too." I got up and put my arms gently around him. "You're not a moron, Kai. You're one of the smartest people I know. You're just naïve when it comes to this stuff."

"Not after this I won't be." He gave me a long squeeze and then pulled out his phone. "I need to report this. It won't take long."

I lay back on his bed, staring at the posters on his wall while he spoke on the phone with the police. I was sure that Kelly and her blog had fueled this fire. But a growing dread was creeping through my mind. Kenji was in Seattle. Christoph was in Germany. Rebecca was grieving. And now Kai was caught up in dealing with a stalker.

It was the kind of thing that Deimos would thrive on.

Deimos. Not long ago he was all I could think of, and then with all the insanity that had happened, I had completely gotten caught up with my "normal" life again. But no more. As soon as I got back from Germany, I was going back on the hunt. I was going to find him and end this.

151

## Chapter Sixteen: The Knife

"Where the hell have you been?" I shouted at Jesse's image in the video chat window on my screen.

"Oh, that's okay, I didn't need that eardrum anyway," Jesse complained as he wiggled his finger in his ear. "Girl, *please*! Why are you shrieking at me? I've been busy, okay?"

"Yeah, well while you and Paul are . . . what did Theresa call it . . . *quarreling*, the world is falling apart."

"We're not quarreling," Jesse sniffed. "We're discussing facts. Don't raise your eyebrow at me."

"Enough already. We have work to do, and since I'm leaving for Germany in twelve hours, it's up to you."

Jesse's face brightened. "Are you going to make it to Berlin? When we lived in Germany, that was my favorite place to go on weekends. There's this one club I snuck into with my friend--"

"Jesse! I'm not going clubbing in Berlin! I'm going there to get Christoph, and besides, my dad is going along."

"Doesn't your dad like to dance? Easy, easy," he laughed. "I'm just messing with you. I wouldn't do it if you didn't get so upset. Your face is almost purple."

I gritted my teeth. "You are so lucky I cannot throw a fireball at you over the Internet. Shut up and pay attention.

While I'm gone, I need you to do some research. We need to find out if there's been any common thread that links the people who've been getting sick."

"What kind of link?"

"I have no idea. Talk to Kenji and Claire and find out if you can get the names of maybe ten or twenty of the victims. Then find out what they have in common. Do they all belong to the same religion? The same political party? Do they work in the same industry? Just see if you can find out anything that might link them."

Jesse frowned. "You're saying you think religion or politics can make people crazy?"

"Yes, but that's an entirely separate conversation," I muttered. "If my suspicion is right and Deimos is behind this, he might be targeting a specific group of people and infecting them."

Jesse shook his head. "I don't see what he stands to gain from it. It's causing suffering, sure, but actual evil? It just doesn't sound right."

"Then why am I the only person in all of Santa Barbara who came down with it?"

"You also went to New York and the Bay Area," he pointed out.

"But I was already having symptoms before that. No, I'm convinced that Deimos is behind this and is using it as a weapon."

Jesse sighed. "Okay, I'll see what I can do. I'll talk to Kenji and Claire. But seriously, Ashlyn, the CDC is already working on this. I don't see why you think we're going to figure out a pattern when they haven't."

"They're not looking for an intentional cause."

Jesse's face suddenly brightened. "Then I'll do one better: I'll look to see who stands to gain from this. I know, I know, you think it must be Deimos getting his jollies by watching people go crazy, but just in case it's not him, I've got some other ideas. Leave everything to me. Go to Germany and bring back our boy."

I closed my laptop and flopped back on my bed. I was so tired, but how in the hell could I sleep with so much to do? Nobody was taking Deimos seriously. It was almost as if he had cast an apathy spell on everyone. Why was I the only person who seemed to remember our primary mission?

A gentle knock on the door made my heart flutter. I pulled myself to my feet as Kai walked into the room, a grave expression on his face.

"What's up?" I asked as I felt the mix of emotions churning inside of him.

"It's Kelly," he began.

"Oh God, don't tell me," I snorted. "She's written a story about how we're actually from another planet. Seriously, Kai, I'm going to kill her if she—"

"Ashlyn!" Kai said, grabbing my arm. He stared helplessly into my eyes for a moment. "She's been attacked. Brutally stabbed. She's not expected to make it through the night."

I let out a long exhale as I felt like all the energy drained out of me. "Oh my God. Do they know who did it?"

"No, not yet. But I've been instructed by the police not to leave town."

My heart started hammering. "What? Why? When did you talk to the police?"

"They came to The Manor a couple hours ago. They managed to recover the weapon, and it happens to have my initials on it. They wanted to know if it was stolen out of my car the night that Debbie smashed my windshield. Guess it's a good thing I reported it as soon as it happened."

"What was a knife doing in your car?"

He frowned. "That's just it. I don't know if it was."

"Kai, you've lost me. What are you saying?"

He slumped onto my bed. "That was a hunting knife my grandfather gave me when I was a kid. I don't remember seeing it for a long time. In fact, I could have sworn I left it at my dad's house when I moved to Minnesota."

I sat next to him and slipped my arm around his waist. "That was a crazy time. You probably put it into your glove box at the last minute or something. It would have made sense, since you were driving across the country alone."

Just then, Rebecca came into the room, a look of deep concern across her face. "What's going on?"

"Kelly's in the hospital. She's been stabbed, and it looks like the attacker used Kai's knife."

Rebecca gasped. "Is she okay?"

"No," Kai said. He looked ashen, and I felt sickening waves of guilt washing over him.

"Then what are we doing sitting here?" she asked in alarm. "Why didn't you call me?"

"We just found out a moment ago," I stammered, but I realized she was right. My first concern had been for Kai. From the moment he'd told me about the knife, I'd given very little thought to the fact that Kelly was near death in a hospital bed. And at that moment I knew the truth: that my hatred for Kelly had become so extreme that a small part of me wanted her to die, and I was telling myself that it was inevitable and conveniently not my fault. I fought back a wave of nausea as Rebecca hurried out of the room.

Kai shook his head. "I don't know what's wrong with me. I should have called Rebecca immediately. Every time I think of my knife tearing into Kelly's body, I feel sick." He picked at a hole that was starting to form in the knee of his jeans. "It's funny, I never did use that knife for hunting. I had no problem fishing, but I couldn't bring myself to kill deer and rabbits. My grandfather used to like to show me pictures of himself with his trophies, bragging about the bear he killed on a trip to Alaska, and I tried to be interested, but I just never understood the appeal. I could tell he was disappointed I didn't turn out to be a hunter like him. Pretty ironic that the knife ended up being used for something so violent anyway."

Kai stared down at his hands, lost in his memories, and suddenly it was as if the world had stopped spinning and was illuminated by bright spotlights, snapping clearly into focus. I gasped, barely able to breathe.

"Ashlyn!" Kai said in alarm. "Are you okay?"

I nodded and swallowed hard. "Better than okay. I think I know what's going on with Christoph."

I jumped to my feet and started shoving the last of my stuff into my suitcase, my mind racing as a strategy began to unfold before me like a roadmap.

## Chapter Seventeen: Tinkerbell

"Are you sure this is the right town?" Dad asked as we took the exit and pulled into the town of Weinheim.

"The sign says it is. Whether Christoph is actually here is another matter entirely." I rubbed my eyes and yawned, trying to fight off the jet lag. It had been a very long flight, followed by a horrible wait to get through customs, and then a mishap where my suitcase almost went to Portugal. Dad had suggested we go to the hotel and take a nap before attempting to find Christoph. But I was not waiting one more second. If my theory was right, Christoph was in trouble, and I needed to find him as soon as humanly possible.

We drove through the little town, winding through small streets lined with adorable shops and restaurants. As we got into the center of town, it looked less and less real, almost like we were at Disneyland. The buildings, which looked like they were made of gingerbread, lined the cobblestone streets from which tall trees sprang with twisted branches stretched toward the sky. People bustled here and there carrying bags of groceries, pulling children along, or being led by enthusiastic dogs. A lush hill of leafy, green trees rose in the background, painting a picture-perfect view straight off a postcard. But I couldn't relax enough to fully appreciate it.

My senses were on full alert as I scanned the face of every person we passed, looking for any sign of Christoph or someone who might be related to him.

Dad pulled the car to a stop in front of an inn. We grabbed our luggage and headed up the steps to the lobby. Inside, we were greeted warmly from behind the reception desk by an elderly man. My dad launched into German conversation with him while I stood back a bit, wondering what they were saying. My dad used to speak German with my grandmother, but I never understood anything they were saying. I wished it had rubbed off on me more, or that I'd been motivated enough to study it in high school. I supposed I could take German as an elective at UCSB, but considering how little time I had for my core subjects, I'd probably need to stick to the easiest classes I could.

My musings over my failing academic career were interrupted when my dad threw his head back and laughed uproariously. The man behind the counter stared at my father in alarm, and then looked at me as if I would be able to explain the joke. Dad stopped laughing enough to say a few more words in German, which caused the man to look wide-eyed at me and then start laughing himself.

"You going to clue me into what's so funny?" I asked, feeling my face getting hot.

"He thought you were my wife," Dad explained. "He couldn't believe I had a daughter as old as you."

"Oh, well thank you. I'm glad I look so old."

"I think it was a compliment to *me*," my dad said, raising his eyebrow. "It's not the first time someone thought I was younger than I am."

"That's great, Dad. But can we discuss your mid-life crisis later and get up to the room? I want to unpack and get going."

He handed me a key. "We're all set, *Fräulein*." He exchanged a few more pleasantries with the man behind the counter while I sprinted up the stairs, anxious to get away from the creepy man who thought I was married to my dad.

The room was unremarkable, with typical basic hotel furniture, but the beds caught my eye. Instead of being covered in the usual ugly floral or striped bedspread, the beds looked unmade, with just a white fitted sheet stretched tightly over each mattress and a folded comforter on top. I poked it a few times; it felt like it was full of feathers.

"Down comforters," my dad said as he entered the room. "You see those everywhere here."

"How come they didn't make the beds?" I asked.

"They believe in airing out the bedding. Makes a lot of sense when you stop to think about it."

"Wish you'd thought of that when you used to always yell at me to make my bed," I mused.

"The unmade bed was the least of the issues with your room. I've never seen such a slob. I'm glad you finally outgrew it. Hmm, the restaurant here looks pretty good," Dad said as he perused a menu that was lying on the table.

"Tell you what," I said through gritted teeth as I opened the window, "you check out places for us to eat tonight, and I'll go do some scouting. If anyone asks where your wife went, tell them I'm sleeping off the jet lag."

"Before you go, I have something for you," he said. He rummaged in his bag for a moment and then pulled out a small silver tool. "It has a pocket knife, scissors, a screwdriver . . . even a file."

I took the tool from his outstretched hand, surprised at how heavy it felt. "It feels rugged."

"It is. I use mine all the time. And in your case, well, just be sure you always have it with you. You just never know."

I pushed it down into the back pocket of my jeans. "Thanks, Dad."

"Don't get lost," he called after me as I disappeared and took off into the sky. "A lot of these buildings look the same."

I soared above the city and sucked in large breaths of the cool air. My brain was so muddled from the long flight and the jet lag that was already taking hold, making me dizzy as everything seemed to shimmer. Traveling with my dad wasn't nearly as weird as I'd thought it would be. We were already settling into our old patterns from when I was a kid. It felt kind of nice, actually.

I flew toward the address Kai had given me for Christoph's parents. It was a little house not too far outside of the town center, on a quiet street lined with slightly more modern-looking houses. I drifted slowly up the street until I came to number twenty-six, a wood and brick building with several windows on each floor and a bright, grass-green door. I flew from window to window, trying to peek in, but they were all shuttered. I flew around the house to the back yard, but it looked as if nobody had been there for a while. I glanced at my phone, which showed the local time as four o'clock. Surely someone would be home soon, I reasoned, and settled onto the roof to wait.

But as the minutes passed, I found myself nodding off. Remembering how disastrous it was the last time I fell asleep while scouting, I decided it was better to head back to the hotel and get some food and a nap. But no sooner had I stood up in preparation to fly from the roof than a car pulled up in front of the house, and out came a man and woman who had to be Christoph's parents. The man was tall and handsome, not as strong-looking as Christoph but definitely solidly built. The woman had a soft expression on her pale face that reminded me so much of Christoph that I suddenly got a lump in my throat. I hadn't realized until that moment just how much I'd missed him.

They went silently into the house and closed the door. I listened through the walls as they moved about, the sounds of clanking and shuffling in the kitchen, and a man's voice on the television speaking rapidly in German. But so far there was no sign of Christoph. I hung around a bit longer until I felt like I couldn't keep my eyes open any longer. I felt sure I'd found the right place and was eager to return and continue scouting. But I wasn't going to rest easy until I actually saw Christoph with my own two eyes.

I turned toward the center of town and headed back to the hotel. I saw the curtain blowing in the breeze, beckoning me back to our room. Those feather beds sounded damn good just then. I would take a nap, have some dinner, and then go back to the house to see whether Christoph had returned. I flew through the window, reappeared, and flopped down on the bed. Exhausted, I closed my eyes and was almost asleep when I was struck by a sickening revelation.

There was someone in my room. And it wasn't my dad.

I snapped open my eyes and looked into the bewildered gaze of a young girl. Her soft, cornflower-blue eyes peeked out from behind long strands of straight, brown hair. She was biting her lip slightly, in a way that reminded me a little of Kai. It gave me a pang of homesickness at the same time as my brain scrambled to come up with a plausible explanation for what she was doing in our room.

Which is when I noticed the horrible truth: this wasn't our room. I had flown in the wrong window.

"Are you Tinkerbell?" she asked.

"Um, what?"

She shrank a bit more behind her hair. "Tinkerbell. Like in Peter Pan."

I sat up slowly. "No, I'm not Tinkerbell. But I think I'm lost, because this doesn't seem to be my room. Where are you from?"

"America," she answered shyly.

"Me too. That explains why you didn't talk to me in German. Um, are your parents here?" I asked looking around nervously.

"They went out for a walk. Willow is in the tub."

"Willow?"

"My big sister." The girl started picking at a scab on her elbow, seeming to forget about me for a moment.

"I tell you what. I better get going before she gets out. I'm sure she wouldn't like finding a stranger in your room."

The girl smiled. "You're not a stranger. You're Tinkerbell."

I smiled back at her. "Maybe so. But now I have to go. Can you do me a favor and close your eyes and count to three?"

She did as I asked and I disappeared. I crept over to the window and reached it just as her eyes snapped open again. Her gaze swept around the room, a perplexed look on her face. Just then, a tall, very thin girl stepped out of the bathroom wearing a towel. Her long, blonde hair hung in wet strands all the way down her back, reminding me somehow of a unicorn's mane.

"What are you doing?" she asked.

"Looking for Tinkerbell. But I think she's hiding."

Willow turned and looked directly at me. She had the same cornflower eyes as her sister, but they seemed sharper, like they saw right through my soul. Her little sister continued to look around the room. Slowly, I drifted into the air and backed out the window, my heart hammering, the older girl's eyes never leaving mine. "I don't think she's hiding," she said in a faraway voice as I drifted into the sky. "I think she flew away."

## Chapter Eighteen: Confessions

"Yes, Michael, I know I'm an idiot, thank you very much. The question is: can some people actually see me when I'm invisible?"

I was on a video call with my unit, giving them a report on our first day. Michael was furious that I'd blown my cover and wasted no time in telling me how stupid I'd been, but John was looking pensive.

"I've never heard of anyone but other Scouts who can see you when you're invisible," John answered. "It sounds like she's too young to be a Scout, so you must have been mistaken. She must have been looking out at the sky."

"I don't think so," I said dubiously. "I could have sworn she was looking right at me."

"Well, it sounds like no harm was done," Kai said. "And the important thing is that you've found Christoph's parents, so it won't be long before you find him."

"If they're actually the right people," Michael scoffed.

"I'm sure of it," I argued. "I'm going back there first thing tomorrow to find out."

"In the meantime, we have some good news," Rebecca broke in. "The police arrested Kai's stalker. Her fingerprints were on the knife, and Kelly identified her from photos as the attacker."

"Oh thank God!" I breathed a huge sigh of relief and smiled at Kai. "I'm so glad you're not going to have to watch your back every second anymore."

"Yeah, you and me both."

"There's more," Rebecca said. "Kenji thinks he's made a breakthrough. He thinks he's isolated the antibody in your blood that will fight off the virus." She looked concerned. "He's going to test it on his parents."

"What? You mean, before testing it on rats or something first?"

"I'm afraid so. He feels they're out of time. Several of the people who first came down with the disease are now in comas. It looks like it's fatal. He feels that it's worth the risk."

I nodded. "I can't say I blame him. I'd rather go down fighting than wait for my parents to die. Speaking of parents, I have to go meet my dad for dinner. I'll call you tomorrow."

I locked eyes with Kai for a moment before ending the call. I missed him so much already. He'd been through a horrible time with my illness and then the stalker and Kelly almost dying. For about the millionth time I wished I could just run away with him somewhere, away from all the madness. But unless I defeated Deimos, that was never going to happen. And first, I had to find Christoph.

The next morning, Dad and I got up early to drive over to Christoph's house. Dad had insisted that there was no point in my hovering around their house all day, and that the best thing to do was to go talk to them.

"But I don't speak German," I argued.

"No, but I do."

"True. I must admit, at the moment that's better than any Soterian power. Go to it, Dad." He parked the car in front of the house, nervously whistling. He looked positively gleeful. I could only imagine how much pent-up frustration he'd had over the years over being shut out of the Soterians, and now here he had his very own mission.

Dad walked briskly up the walk and rapped loudly on the front door. A moment later Christoph's mom answered. My dad immediately launched into a lengthy explanation of something or other while she listened patiently. Finally, she invited him in, and I watched the door close behind him.

I flew out the window and went to hover near the house. I heard some conversation between my dad and Christoph's mom, followed by the sound of heavy footsteps. A man's voice, which I assumed belonged to Christoph's dad, joined the conversation. They all chatted for a while before I finally heard the sound of them getting to their feet and walking to the front door. I flew back through the car window and waited anxiously for Dad to return. Finally, the front door opened and Dad emerged. He turned and shook their hands before finally heading back to the car.

"Well, what happened?" I asked as he started the engine and pulled away.

"I told them I was from the university and was concerned about their son's absence from school. They told me he'd been going through a tough time because of a death in the family and that they're trying to convince him to return to school."

"But where IS he?" I asked impatiently.

"They said he left a few days ago and didn't say where he was going, but that they suspect he went to his house in the mountains. His grandfather left it to him along with all his money and possessions."

"Where is the house?"

Dad pulled out a map and pointed to a point he'd circled. "Here, in this little town."

"Got it. Good work, Dad. You would have made a good Keeper."

His face clouded. "Unfortunately, the job was already taken."

I immediately regretted my words. "Mom loved you, you know. She really did."

"It all worked out fine," he said dismissively. "I wonder how Evelyn is getting along with the remodeling."

"Don't be surprised if your living room is fuchsia when you get home."

We drove in silence for a while, looking at the beautiful scenery of the southern Germany countryside, lost in our own thoughts. So Christoph's grandfather left him everything instead of giving it all to Christoph's dad, his only son. That fit neatly with my theory about what was going on, but I didn't have the whole situation figured out yet. I wouldn't know more until I talked to Christoph.

An hour later, we were winding our way through narrow, twisting streets until we reached the top of one especially perilous road that was nothing but gravel for the last fifty yards. Perched at the apex of this slope was a sweet little Bavarian house of brown brick, white walls criss-crossed with wooden slats, and windows framed in green. It looked very small from the outside, like it contained only a couple of rooms, and the view over the top of the vast forest of tall, green trees was spectacular. As we inched toward the house, the car's tires crunching loudly on the gravel, my heart was hammering. What was I going to say to Christoph? Was I going to be persuasive enough to convince him to come back to Santa Barbara, to Rebecca? What if I failed her and the rest of my unit? I took a deep breath and decided that failure was simply not an option. I had to convince him to come back.

"Dad, I think it'll be best if I talk to him first, and then I'll call you in, okay?"

"Sure. I'll wait in the car." He pulled out a magazine and started reading. It reminded me so much of the times Kai had waited for me while I was scouting. A lump of gratitude rose in my throat for both of them, the two most important men in my life.

I opened the car door, stretched, and slowly approached the house. I knocked gently on the front door, the rough wood and peeling paint scratchy on my knuckles. I waited and then knocked again, this time continuing to knock until I heard movement inside the house followed by heavy footsteps. I instinctively took a step back, and a moment later the door swung open, and Christoph's form filled the entryway. I bit back a gasp as I studied his face. He looked even worse than Rebecca had. His face was drawn, and his skin looked almost grey. He was still big and beefy, but he looked thinner than I'd ever seen him. Worst of all was the haunted look in his eyes, as if he was expecting a ghost to appear before him at any moment.

He stared at me, dumbfounded, for several moments. "Ashlyn?"

"Hey, Christoph." My voice sounded shaky. "I'm so glad I've found you. Can we talk for a while?"

"What are you doing here?" He seemed frozen in the doorway.

"I've come to talk to you, that's all." He still didn't move, so I swallowed hard. "Um, could I possibly get a drink of water?"

That lit a spark in him. "Yes, yes, come in." He stepped inside and I followed him into a little room. There was a wooden table and two chairs next to a tiny kitchen. A sofa

167

with a pillow and blanket on it was pushed up against the side wall. The room was dark and gloomy.

"So this is where you've been staying, huh? The view is incredible from here." I walked to a window and pushed back the dusty curtains, flooding the room with a pale light. "Wow, it looks like this window hasn't been cleaned in a hundred years. Were you planning on keeping it this way?"

He walked slowly toward me and held out a glass of water. I took it from him and sipped it. It was cool and fresh. "This tastes like it came straight from a stream. Pretty amazing spot." I sat down at the table, and he followed my lead. "So how have you been? We all miss you a lot."

He continued to stare at me. "I'm not coming back," he said at last.

"Yeah, I kind of figured that out. I'd like to hear why."

His gaze dropped. "I just can't. I don't belong there. This is where my home is."

I cocked my head to the side. "Really? I thought you wanted to move to New York. I was just there, visiting Rebecca, and I could really picture you there." At the sound of Rebecca's name, a wave of pain crossed his face, and I thought he was going to cry. I put my hand gently on his. "Christoph, why don't you tell me what's going on?"

He got heavily to his feet and went into the kitchen. "How is Rebecca?"

"How do you think she is? Look, I'm not here to make you feel guilty. I can see that you're already completely torn up inside. But if you think she's somehow better off without you, you couldn't be more wrong. She's bad, Christoph. Really bad. I've never seen her like this. She almost dropped out of school."

I could feel the horror rising in his chest. "She can't do that! She has to become a doctor and help people."

"It's kind of hard to do that when your heart is smashed in a million pieces. She'll never be the same without you."

"I should never have asked her to marry me," he wailed. "I should never have dated her. I should have left her alone so she could find someone who deserved her. I can't stand it that I've made her suffer. Is that all we ever do?"

"By 'we' I assume you mean you and your grandfather. Am I right?"

Christoph stared hard at me. "What do you mean?"

"I mean that this is about your grandfather's past, isn't it? That you found out something about him that you can't live with, because you think you're just like him."

He looked like he was going to be sick. "His blood is my blood. I spent all my summers with him, and he always told me I was just like him. He left me everything, because he wanted me to carry on his tradition."

There was a dangerous tension emanating from Christoph, as if he were going to explode. His anguish was as bad as anything I'd felt from Rebecca, but there was also a rage in him I'd never felt before. "Christoph, you have every right to be angry at him, but not at yourself. His past is his, not yours."

"It's not true!" he shouted. "He wrote the things I said, the things I did when I was a boy. I found his journals with his other . . . trophies." He glanced toward a closed door.

"I'd like to take a look, to help you sort through this. You need a friend right now. I'm not going to sugar-coat it, Christoph. If you were a monster, I'm going to say so, but only so you can face it and make amends. Not so you can spend your life here rotting away, which isn't going to make anything better." I moved toward the door, hesitating just a moment before I opened it. I could hear his heart pounding across the room.

I turned the knob and stepped into a small room with a single bed, a small dresser, a reading table, and a bookshelf. Boxes were stacked in the corners. I moved slowly through the room, stepping over the items strewn across the floor. Swastikas seemed to pop out from all over the place like cockroaches. It was amazing how such a simple symbol could say so much, have such power. I was certain that Deimos was in his full glory during that era. In fact, it seemed likely that he was Hitler himself.

I picked up a journal that was lying open on the desk. It was all in German, none of which I could read, but I saw Christoph's name mentioned. I walked back into the living room, where Christoph was still rooted to the same spot. "Would you translate this for me?" I asked.

He hesitantly took it from me as if I were handing him a dead rat, and then he began to read in a quiet voice. "'Christoph continues to make me proud. He told me today how he and his friends stole a Jewish boy's money and that he was saving to buy a special gun that he would use to hunt them. He asked me how much money he would need to buy the right gun. I am happy that Christoph is not like his father and is like me instead. One day he will inherit my fortune, which started in the same way.'" My blood froze in my veins as I heard him read. I had already figured out that his grandfather was a Nazi, but I couldn't imagine how Christoph himself could ever have subscribed to the same beliefs.

He closed the journal and looked hard at me. "You see? I am just like him. I can't escape what I've done, what he did. And now I have his house, and his money, that he got by killing people. How could I ever be with good people again, knowing what I am? How could I even look at Rebecca? My grandfather could have killed people in her family."

"Why did he hate Jews so much?" I asked.

"He thought they were the reason he had such a hard time finding work. And then he found work with the Nazi party."

"Do you know if anyone else in your family felt the same way?"

He shook his head. "In his journal he said it was a problem between him and his parents. They didn't like what he was doing and left Germany when Hitler rose to power. And my father never agreed with my grandfather. That was why my grandfather was so happy when I was born and was just like him."

"But you're not just like him, don't you see that? You listened to him when you were young and impressionable. He was very good to you, and you loved him and trusted him, so when he said you were just like him you believed him and tried to make him proud. But I'm guessing it didn't last long, did it?"

Christoph looked down. "When I was seven years old, I beat up a boy and took his money. Later I found out that it had been to buy a present for his grandfather. For the first time, I thought about what I was doing, that these boys had grandfathers they loved and wanted to impress, too. I changed to a different school so I could start over. I never wanted to hurt anyone again."

"And that's the difference! You realized what you were doing, and you stopped. You see? It wasn't your destiny or any crap like that. Your grandfather was a sad, angry man, and your parents were crazy for letting you spend time with him."

"They didn't know. I knew they didn't believe the same things as my grandfather, and so it was just our secret. I never told them, or anyone." Christoph paced around the room, breathing hard. The anger and shame and turmoil roiling inside of him was almost more than I could bear.

"The important thing is that it's all in the past. You have made a new life for yourself in the United States. With us. We love you, and we need you back. Rebecca most of all."

Christoph stiffened, then turned resolutely away. "No. I can't go back. That's final."

I was about to keep arguing when there was a knock and the sound of the front door swinging open. My dad's voice called out from the entryway. "Ashlyn?"

Christoph looked horrified. "Who is that?"

"My dad. Come meet him."

"No. I don't want to see anyone." Christoph stood firmly, his jaw set in a stubborn square.

"Look, you either walk into that room or I'm going to pick you up and fly you there. And you know I can." I grabbed his hand, apparently surprising him into submission, and pulled him into the front room.

"Dad, this is Christoph Voight. Christoph, this is my dad, Robert Woods."

"*Angenehm*, Christoph. Sorry to barge in, but could I use your bathroom?"

"Of course," Christoph said. In an instant, his whole demeanor changed from slumped resignation to alert hospitality. "Would you like some water, perhaps?"

"*Ein Bier, bitte*, if you have it," Dad replied as he headed into the bathroom.

"Dad just loves German beer," I said with a smile.

Christoph reached into the cupboard and pulled out a mug. "Why is he here? Why didn't you tell me he was with you?"

"I wanted to talk to you first. Dad knows about the Soterians," I added. "Turns out my mom was an Empath. I

172

found out last week after I went insane and burned down my father's house while I was trying to kill Kai."

"What?!" Christoph's eyes bugged wide. "What has been happening?"

"A lot, but sadly not enough. We really need you back."

Dad came out of the bathroom and joined us in the kitchen. "Ah, that looks perfect. *Prosit!*" He took the mug from Christoph and drank a long swig. "So Christoph, Ashlyn tells me you're their Sentry. Or were their Sentry. They're pretty short right now, with the other Sentry out of commission. Not that I understand all this Soterian business, but it seems like a bad idea for two units to be without any kind of defense."

Christoph looked back and forth between us and swallowed hard. He ran his hand through his hair and stared past us at his grandfather's room, looking lost. "I don't know what to do with those . . . things."

"I'll be happy to help you build a bonfire. I've gotten rather good at burning stuff down lately."

"I can vouch for that," my Dad said with a frown. "You should see my kitchen."

"I'll donate the money to a Jewish charity," Christoph said resolutely. "And the house."

"Sounds like a good idea. Just keep enough money to start your preschool in Manhattan."

Christoph looked hard at me. "She'll never take me back. I can't ask her to."

"She's already forgiven you," I said. "Just get your ass back there and start making amends."

Later that night, as we sat in front of the bonfire, and Christoph threw the last artifact of his dark history into the flames, I watched him carefully out of the corner of my eye.

His feelings had been much calmer over the last few hours, and a strength and resolve was building in him. But there was still an underlying guilt mixed with terror. I knew that feeling all too well; I'd felt it every time I'd had to make amends with Kai, and every time I awoke from one of my dreams about Michael. I didn't envy the hell that he and Rebecca were going to have to endure to repair their relationship.

## Chapter Nineteen: Reconciliation

"Are you ready?" I asked.

Christoph breathed deeply. His emotions were like a snowstorm, and his face was decidedly green. "I'm not sure," he said in a shaky voice.

I took his hand. "It's okay. I've been in this situation before. Well, without the Nazi grandfather, but you get my point. I know what you're going through, and it's going to be okay. She'll forgive you. Remember when you fixed the window I blew up?"

A trace of a smile crossed his lips. "Kai was very calm."

"And Rebecca will be, too. I've already spoken to her, and she's anxious to see you."

We sat watching as the last of the passengers disembarked from the plane. The flight attendants stood at the front, eyeing us curiously, obviously wondering what the hell we were doing. I gave Christoph a little poke. "The plane isn't going to turn around. One-way trip. Let's go."

He heaved a great sigh and slowly stood, easily hooking his large duffle bag and my carry-on case from the overhead bin with single fingers. I followed him slowly down the aisle, wishing he wouldn't look quite so much like he was marching to his death. But then I remembered how I'd felt when Michael forced me to go see Kai after my blow up, and I remembered to be compassionate. I was confident Rebecca wouldn't give him a hard time, but this wasn't going to be easy.

As we walked through the Los Angeles airport to the baggage claim area, my eyes automatically scanned every face I saw. I wouldn't put it past Deimos to be here for this little reunion. Three Soterians with their guards down, distracted by the drama between Rebecca and Christoph, made us a tempting target. I almost wished he'd take the bait and show himself.

As we passed the security gates, I felt Christoph stiffen, and I followed his gaze to Rebecca and Kai. My heart began to race. I was getting more and more used to not seeing Kai every day, but being halfway around the world had made it much harder. As Kai and I embraced, I saw that Rebecca was still hanging back. She looked as pale and thin as before, but there was now a fire in her eyes. Christoph hesitated a moment, then strode over to her, nearly knocking down several people in his path. He stopped right before he got to her.

"I'm sorry," he said in a hoarse whisper. "I'm so sorry."

Suddenly, it was as if the world had turned red. The pain and rage I felt coming from Rebecca was unlike anything I'd ever felt, even at my most insane moments. She let out an animal scream, causing everyone in the terminal to turn and look, and she started flailing and beating on Christoph with all her might. Kicking, screaming, pounding his face over and over again with her fists, tearing his shirt to ribbons. He just stood there in horror, her blows bouncing off of him like he was made of rubber. Kai and I grabbed her and pulled her back.

"Let go of me! Let go of me! I'm going to kill him! I'm going to fucking KILL him!" She was screaming so loudly I thought my eardrums would burst. Thank God my Alchemist powers had kicked in and given me the strength of a Sentry, because the adrenaline coursing through her veins made her incredibly strong and impossible for a normal person to control. Her left hand was hanging at an odd angle, and I knew she'd broken her wrist. While Kai talked quietly to Christoph, I forced Rebecca backwards into a chair and onto my lap, where I held her securely, pouring healing into her while she flailed about and continued screaming. Finally, she became quieter, her hand popped back into a normal position, and she took deeper breaths.

"It's okay," I whispered. "It's all going to be okay now."

"Let me go," she said in a low voice.

"Bec, just stay with me a minute longer . . . "

"No, let me go NOW." I dropped my arms and let her jump to her feet. She ran over to Christoph, who looked so scared and wounded I thought he would fall over. She ran at him full force, but instead of beating on him, she threw her arms around him and began sobbing, tears running down her face and soaking the tattered remains of his shirt. He looked stunned for a moment, then put his arms gently around her. He kissed her tentatively on top of her head and pulled her in closer as tears flooded his eyes.

"Come on," Kai said. "Let's give them some privacy."

"In the middle of the airport?"

He walked over to Christoph. "Call us when you're ready to go. Take all the time you need."

Before Christoph could respond, Kai clapped him on the shoulder, took my arm, and led me toward baggage claim. I stumbled a few times, feeling very unsteady after the long flight, the endless worrying about Rebecca's reaction, which

177

was both better and much worse than I had expected, and healing her during her flip-out. All I wanted was to take a hot bubble bath and crawl into bed, but I knew I had a long night of processing ahead once Rebecca was ready to talk to me.

Kai and I settled into a café and drank coffee as we waited for Christoph and Rebecca. I told him how Dad and I had helped Christoph clear out his grandfather's place and then took him back to his parents' house. I'd stayed in their guest room that night so I could keep an eye on Christoph and make sure he didn't run off again, and I spent most of the night listening to him pacing in his room above me. The next morning, Dad had driven north to finish off his trip inspecting his properties, and I'd spent the next couple of days helping Christoph get everything in order so he could come back with me to the U.S.

"How did his parents take the news?" Kai asked me as he sipped his coffee.

"They were very sweet to him. His mother cried a lot; she'd had no idea that Christoph had been carrying around so much guilt. His father had suspected something was up, but Christoph just wouldn't talk to him."

"Poor guy," Kai said. "I hope Rebecca forgives him quickly."

I smiled sadly. "Not everyone is as understanding as you are, Kai."

"I mean when she hears about his past."

Images of Christoph's grandfather in Nazi uniform popped unbidden into my mind. "I'm sure she'll be able to move beyond it, but I'm much more worried about her parents. If Rebecca and Christoph are still going to get married, they have an uphill battle to convince them that he's not going to run out on her again, let alone telling them that his grandfather was a Nazi." I got a shiver just thinking about the look that would be on Susan's and Bob's faces during *that* particular conversation. "Speaking of Nazis, how is Kelly doing? Sorry, that was insensitive," I said at the look of concern that crossed Kai's face. "It's been a long couple of weeks."

"She's recovering well physically, thanks to Rebecca's healing. But emotionally? She's still kind of a mess. Rebecca said she's just kind of checked out, doesn't respond that much. Except she does wake up screaming a lot."

I looked at him over my coffee cup. "I'm sorry. This must really suck for you."

He peered back at me. "I know I shouldn't feel guilty. God knows she brought this on herself if anyone did. But, I don't know . . . I can't help feeling like there's more to this than we know. That somehow we're responsible."

My stomach lurched. "You mean that it has something to do with the Soterians. With Deimos?" I asked in a low whisper. Reflexively, I scanned the room again, reaching out with my feelings to try to sense his presence.

Kai held my gaze and finally nodded. "Yes."

My heart was hammering. "So you've finally decided I'm not just being overly paranoid."

He shook his head. "I never said you were. I just keep hoping the day won't come . . . that somehow we can delay the inevitable." He took my hand tightly in his. "We're not ready. Legend or whatever says that you're the only one who can go up against him because you're an Alchemist, but you're still recovering from being sick, and we don't know how you got infected in the first place. Plus, we have no idea who he is or exactly how you're going to defeat him once we do find him. We're just not ready for you to take him on."

A small laugh escaped my lips. "You mean you're not ready for me to take him on."

"That too," he conceded. His eyes bored into me. "I'm not ready to lose you."

I pulled away. "You should have more faith in me, Kai. Did it ever occur to you that maybe I was called to this because I can actually beat him?"

"I do have faith in you. If anyone can do it, it's you. But we've been told over and over that he can't be defeated. And you've become so obsessed with finding him. I just want you to spend more time thinking about what you're going to do once you do find him."

I laughed again. "And here I thought I was the one who always overplanned everything." I leaned in closer. "Don't worry about me, Kai. I didn't know how to create a fireball, or harness my Warrior or Sentry powers . . . it all just happened, and just in time to save your life. I think the same thing is going to happen once I finally go up against Deimos. Another gene will trigger or whatever and I'll have the strength to take him on."

Just then, Kai's phone beeped. "It's Christoph," he said, reading the text. "They're ready to meet us and go home."

"Excellent," I said, getting to my feet. "Text him back while I clear the table."

I picked up our cups and headed over to the counter, all the while trying hard to fight back the tears that were welling up inside of me. I hated lying to Kai, hated it more than anything. But I couldn't tell him the truth: that I had gone up against Deimos so many times in my dreams and was never able to defeat him. I did have some small hope that something would come to me once I actually confronted him, but it was more a story I told myself than anything else. If I thought about it too much, let myself really go there, I would know the truth—that there was no defeating Deimos. And if I ever let myself fully believe that, I was as good as dead.

We met up with Rebecca and Christoph and walked in silence to the car. They were holding hands and looked like they'd reached some sort of resolution, but there was still a deep sadness mingled with their relief and joy at being together again. Still, it was a major step in the right direction. And as we drove west, out of the haze of the Los Angeles smog, through the farms, and finally along the ocean, I felt their sorrow drain steadily and become replaced by so much love it made my heart hurt. I took Kai's hand in mine, feeling the warmth and love emanating from him, and we drove silently all the way back to Santa Barbara, basking in the love that was swirling around all four of us.

## Chapter Twenty: Mutations

"I've got it!" Jesse yelled into the phone. "I swear, this time I've got it."

I sighed. "What have you got, and how contagious is it?"

"Shut up and listen. I think I've figured out who's responsible for the virus."

There was a long pause as he waited to let this statement sink in. Unfortunately, the dramatic effect was a bit ruined by the fact that this was his third pronouncement that he'd found the culprit.

"Who is it this time? Aliens? Wait, I know! Zombies!"

"What part of 'shut up' don't you understand? Look, we know the virus has been found in people's intestines, right? So we've been assuming it's something they ate, like how people get mad cow disease from eating meat. But what if we're looking at it from the . . . wrong direction?" He finished his question in a dramatic undertone, and I bit my lip.

"Jesse, you might be on to something!" I whispered darkly. "I mean, I would never have thought that someone would be putting viruses on *toilet paper*. My God! Your genius is beyond words."

The phone clicked as he hung up on me, and I burst out laughing. Poor Jesse. He'd been trying so hard to come up with an answer, but without any leads there was no recon to do, no paths to follow. So he'd taken to sitting around his apartment dreaming up wild possibilities, each hypothesis more ridiculous than the last. The fact that he was now considering tainted toilet tissue spoke volumes about how desperate he was for an answer. Paul had even sent me a concerned email about the conspiracy websites Jesse was starting to read, but I advised him that it would all blow over as soon as we found an answer.

But the knowledge that we were no closer to finding a solution settled heavily on my shoulders. I'd spent so much time and energy getting Christoph home, and I guess I thought that if we were all together again, somehow we could move forward with the mission. But the truth was that nothing had changed at all. It had been three weeks since we got back from Germany, and we weren't any closer to figuring out who and what was behind the epidemic. The only silver lining was that I had managed to catch up on all my classes and hadn't been thrown out of school.

My reverie was interrupted by a knock at the door, driving all gloomy thoughts of virus-laden toilet paper out of my head. I strode into the living room and pulled open the front door to see Toby and Ryan standing there.

"Hey!" Toby said. "There's a pool tournament at the pub tonight. Do you want to join us?"

I smiled. "Ryan, do you think you're up to having your ass kicked again?"

"That was a long time ago," he scoffed. "I've been practicing. What do you say? And hellooo," Ryan said slipping past me into the living room before I could respond. I turned and saw that Lili had come out of her room to see what was going on. She was wearing form-fitting yoga pants and a lycra top that pushed her breasts together, forming a deep line of cleavage. "You're Lili, right? Don't think we've met. I'm Ryan."

"Hey Ryan," she said, looking slightly amused. "I've heard a lot about you."

"It's almost all true. You have incredibly beautiful eyes," he murmured.

"Really?" She covered her eyes with her palms. "What color are they?"

Ryan hesitated. "Uh, I mean . . ."

She moved her hands down to her chest and covered her breasts. "NOW what color are they?"

Ryan turned scarlet, and Lili shot him a playful look.

"Lili!" I said, unable to stop myself. "We're heading downtown to a pool tournament. Ryan has assured us he's going to take home the trophy this time. Want to join us?" I caught Ryan looking horrified out of the corner of my eye, but a delighted smile crossed Lili's face.

"I'd love to. One sec while I go put on panties."

Ryan blushed furiously again, and I was just able to call out, "We'll wait outside!" before Toby and I ran out onto the walkway and burst out laughing.

"It's pretty damn satisfying to see Ryan finally meet his match," I said when I could breathe again. "But I have a feeling once he gets a few beers in him he'll be able to hold his own."

Toby shook his head. "No doubt. I wonder why we didn't introduce them sooner?"

"Probably because he's always too busy dating the woman of the week. Shhh, here they come."

True to form, Ryan had recovered nicely and was already deep in conversation with Lili. I noticed that he was taking care to look her in the eyes as she talked.

As we headed toward the parking lot, I saw a light in Kelly's apartment. I felt a wave of guilt as I realized I hadn't thought about her in over a week. Rebecca had been visiting her regularly and was most certainly responsible both for saving her life the night she was stabbed and for her excellent recovery. I didn't know whether Kelly appreciated it or not, but Rebecca had become a true friend to her. I wondered how Rebecca could put up with her.

Just at that moment, Rebecca walked out of Kelly's apartment and looked up at me. I waved at her, and she pointed to the parking lot. I hurried ahead of Toby and the others and met her at the bottom of the stairs.

"How's it going, Bec?" I asked. "Is Kelly finally treating you like a human being?"

"She's not that bad, Ashlyn. I know the two of you have not exactly seen eye to eye, but she's been through a lot. She deserves our compassion."

"Well then, you're just the Empath for the job," I said. "Come to the pool tournament with us? Ryan is trying to impress Lili." I glanced over my shoulder at Ryan and Lili as they descended the stairs. Lili definitely seemed intrigued, and I silently placed odds on how long it took them to leave the pool tournament and race back to jump into bed together.

Rebecca smiled and nodded. "You're right, I don't give it more than three hours myself. But as much as I'd like to stay and watch the show, I've got work to do, and then I'm supposed to meet Christoph later when he and Michael get back from LA."

"Are you guys doing okay?"

She nodded. "Yes, I think so. It's been an interesting time, to say the least."

I put my arms around her. "I'm really proud of the way you guys are handling everything. Seriously, if you can get past this, you're pretty much good to go."

She squeezed me and then pulled away. "You might be right. Anyway, gotta run."

I watched her walk up the stairs, remarking to myself on how much older she looked. I couldn't believe I'd met her less than two years ago. Time is so weird, I thought. We think of it as being a constant force—unchanging and predictable—but our perception of it is so elastic. Why does it seem to stand still at times and at other times it moves like lightning? It was like the time I'd gotten a virus on my computer. Everything would be working normally, and then it would gradually slow down until it was crawling. I couldn't understand why my virus software hadn't caught it. Maybe the virus had mutated.

I felt the world spin slightly.

I pulled out my phone and called Jesse. It rang several times before he finally answered with a short, "Well?"

"It was an accident," I whispered. "The virus mutated. What drugs are being given to the patients?"

"I already checked that out. They're on all kinds of shit. Not one specific drug."

"Okay, then, have any hot new antiviral drugs come out recently?"

There was a pause as I heard him typing in the background. "Drexipan came out a year ago. But its sales have been fairly flat." I heard him typing more quickly. "Well, look at this. It looks like they've just launched a marketing campaign touting it as a precautionary drug for health care workers to help them avoid coming down with the virus."

"Interesting. And who makes Drexipan?"

There was a pause. "Biotrek."

"Video chat in five. Get Claire and Kenji on the line, too." I hung up and turned to Toby, who was waiting on the walkway to the parking lot. "Sorry, Toby, but a friend needs my help. Rain check?"

"Sure. And be sure to tell Claire that if she needs anything, I'm right here," he said with a smile. I watched him turn and follow Ryan and Lili out of the complex before I raced upstairs.

Ten minutes later, I was in a video conference with Jesse, Claire, and Kenji. I noticed he looked even worse than the last time I'd seen him.

"I buy the mutation hypothesis," Kenji said. "It explains why the drugs aren't working. But what I don't get is why Biotrek would create a virus like this in the first place, if all they intended to do was treat the healthcare workers. It's not a big enough market to justify the risk."

"Health care workers today," Jesse answered, "but pretty soon parents and school teachers and everyone else will want to take Drexipan, too."

"I wonder," Claire said. "Maybe they intended for Drexipan to cure the virus, but after it mutated, they just switched gears and sold it as a preventative agent."

"And then they had a real crisis on their hands," Jesse mused. He stared at me. "It wasn't Deimos after all. It was just a greedy bunch of assholes trying to make a buck."

"Don't be so sure," I said. "There's still no explanation of how I got infected. I think it's highly coincidental that both Kenji and I were put out of commission by this. Kenji, if this hadn't happened, what would you be working on right now?"

He looked pensive for a moment. "I was working on my thesis. I was supposed to graduate this year."

"And what would you do when you graduated?"

"I've had a few offers already. One was . . . " he paused. "A biotech firm called SymLife. They're a competitor of Biotrek."

"Wow!" Claire said. "But Ashlyn, that doesn't explain why you were infected."

"Unless you had some stellar job options you forgot to tell us about," Jesse said with a wry smile.

"Exactly. The only reason to target me is because I'm an Alchemist. So although Biotrek is behind this and is using the virus to their advantage, they're obviously in bed with Deimos, who is also using it to his advantage."

"So what's our next step?" Claire asked.

"I have some news there," Kenji said. "It's preliminary, and I don't want to get our hopes up. As you know, I've been isolating parts of Ashlyn's blood sample and giving them to my parents. Well, I finally isolated a protein that was present in almost undetectable amounts. So small that I missed it at first. But I finally got enough to administer to my parents, so I gave it to them tonight. I'm going to visit them again in the morning to see how they're doing."

"Fantastic!" I said. "Kenji, I think you should contact SymLife. Tell them you have a possible cure to the virus that you'll need to put into large-scale production immediately."

"And ask for a higher salary than they previously offered you," Jesse chimed in. "Meanwhile, I'll investigate Biotrek." He sounded thrilled to be on the right track at last.

"I'll fill in the rest of the Soterians," Claire said.

"And I'll keep trying to figure out how they managed to infect me so that we can stop it before it spreads any further," I added. "It doesn't seem to spread from person to person or our whole unit would have come down with it by now."

"Or at least Kai, since you can't seem to keep your tongue out of his mouth," Jesse said.

"Sounds like we've all got plenty to focus on," I said, ignoring him. "Kenji, call us as soon as you've visited your parents, okay?"

We hung up, and I sat back on the bed. I had racked my brains a million times to try to figure out how I'd been infected. Now, it was time to try a different approach. I crossed my legs, closed my eyes, and started following my breath, allowing the thoughts to flow in and out of my mind. At first, they were bouncing all of over the place, but soon I settled into the rhythm of my breathing and found the quiet, calm place where everything just seemed to flow. Memories passed by like leaves on a stream. Blowing up Kai's amp . . . my former boss going mad . . . skiing with my unit and Christoph falling under the snow . . . Rebecca's depression . . . my trip to New York and the man who burst through the gallery window . . . the trip to Germany . . . Kelly's obsession with ruining Kai's reputation, and the crazed fan who stabbed her. I focused on letting these images pass before me without trying to grab onto them and figure anything out.

And sure enough, I didn't figure anything out.

I took a deep breath and stretched, trying to let go of the frustration and panic that threatened to well up inside of me. Time was running out, but my only option was to be patient, because the more I forced it, the more elusive the answer would be. I tried to take another step back, but the only pattern I saw in all of these events was obsession and madness leading to awful things. I picked up my goddess figurine and stared into her face as I tried to clear my mind. "Come on, Fuchi. Help me out."

Just then, my phone buzzed, and I heard Kai's beautifully resonant voice on the other end. "Hey, Kai. What's up?"

"I just got off the phone with Kelly. We talked about her blog, and she agreed to let it go."

"Well, it's about time she saw reason," I said. "But what made her change her mind?"

"I think she just saw how negative her blog was and how that was attracting the crazies. She actually apologized to me for what she'd written. She admitted that she was just being vindictive."

"Um, did she come down with the virus, too? That just doesn't sound like Kelly at all."

"I know, but I think this experience really shook her up. She's determined to act human again."

I shook my head. "I'm not dropping my guard. She's up to something. Mark my words."

"Maybe, but she's taken her blog down. Check it out for yourself."

We hung up, and I felt myself fuming. Why was everyone being so nice to Kelly? She had been so rude to Rebecca when we first arrived, and now they were like best friends. She had tried to ruin Kai's life as well as mine, and here he was being all forgiving, as if nothing had happened. I remembered that time she watched me rescue the kid who was drowning, and the look on her face as she saw me use my powers to bring him into shore. As if she had figured it out. . .

As if she already knew.

I put Fuchi back on my bookshelf and headed for the door.

## Chapter Twenty-One: A Disturbing Note

"How long have you known?"

Kelly hugged the blanket a little tighter around her shoulders and settled back into her chair, and I tried to let go of the horror I felt that I was actually sitting in her apartment having a civil conversation with the bitch who had made my life miserable for the last two years.

"I suspected there was something different about you right away," she replied.

"Why was that exactly?"

"Oh, let's see," she said, her voice dripping with sarcasm. "There was the time you woke up on the walkway outside your apartment, and the time you swam faster than was humanly possible. And all the weird stuff Tracy told me about you and Rebecca."

"Tracy?"

Kelly looked down her nose at me. "Your former roommate who almost OD'd? Remember her?"

"Yes, Kelly, I remember her. I just didn't realize she knew what was going on."

"I wouldn't say she knows what's going on. I don't pretend to understand it, either. I just knew there was something weird about you guys, and then when David approached me—"

"David?" I broke in. "Skinny computer geek with an annoying smirk on his face all the time?"

"That's the one. He told me that you and Rebecca were involved in anti-government stuff and selling drugs. He said the best thing I could do was to try to get you busted, that you were going to bring Kai down."

"Excuse me for calling bullshit on your story, but your blog posts didn't exactly seem to be about trying to protect Kai."

"Of course not. By that time I figured he was involved in the same stuff you were."

"Got it. So you were doing this out of the goodness of your heart? To protect the students of UCSB and the general populace from a group of anarchist drug dealers, who just happened to be led by your ex-boyfriend's new girlfriend?"

"Is that why you came over here? To mock me? Because frankly, I haven't been through enough crap in the last two weeks and really need your shit on top of everything else."

I felt myself soften involuntarily, which irritated me even more. Stupid Empath powers. Sometimes I wished I could turn it all off on command. "Fine, I'm sorry. Just tell me what you know and I'll be out of your hair."

"All I know is that you and Rebecca are involved in some weird, secret experiments that give you special powers. And that it's for the greater good or something. That's why I stopped the blog. I haven't heard from David for months, anyway."

"That's because he's in prison," I explained. "For his involvement in a drug ring."

Kelly frowned. "So why was he trying to set you up?"

"Let's just say we have a lot of enemies who don't want us to succeed in our mission." I got to my feet. "Thanks for the information. It would help us a lot if you just forgot all about this. And if David or anyone else contacts you about us again, let us know." I turned to leave, then stopped. "And by the way, I'm happy you're not dead."

"Great. Glad to hear it."

I walked out of her apartment, closed the door, and breathed a sigh of relief. That was awkward as hell, but it explained a lot, and I felt much better. Kelly was a manipulative idiot, but she wasn't truly malicious. In the end, she was just doing what she thought was right. I wondered if she'd have more of a part to play before this was all over.

At the sound of familiar footsteps, I turned to see Kai coming down the stairs, his guitar bag slung over his shoulder. "Well?" he asked.

"You were right. She knew something was up all along. She's vague on the details, and I didn't go to any trouble to enlighten her. But she knows now to stay the hell away from David and any of Deimos' other henchmen."

"She knows about Deimos?"

"Not by name, no." I took Kai's hand. "Are you off to band practice?"

"Yeah." He paused. "It's our last one before we head out on tour."

My stomach clenched. "I kind of forgot about that. I mean, on purpose. I'm not ready for you to go."

He pulled me to him and touched his forehead to mine. "I know. I wish I could stay here and help you."

"I don't. This is what you've always wanted. I would never wish that you'd miss out on an opportunity like this, no matter how bad it's going to suck for me to be left behind."

Kai smiled. "I have a feeling you're going to handle it a lot better than Michael. He's been moping around for days."

"You're probably right. I'll do my best to keep him occupied without killing him."

"I'll bet you will," Kai said with a smirk.

I smacked him playfully. "Don't you start with that."

"I'm just teasing you, Ashlyn. I trust you. Completely."

I put my arms around him. "I trust you, too. Almost completely. That was a joke!" I insisted as he pulled away. "Really. I do trust you."

"Trust him to do what?" a voice asked. I turned to see Marlowe approaching us, moving with her usual fluid, cat-like grace. Before I could answer, she held out a bag to Kai. "Kai, could you load up our stuff? I want to ask Ashlyn something."

"Sure thing," he said. He took the bag from her and headed for the parking lot. Marlowe watched him walk away for a few moments before turning to me.

"Ashlyn, I want you to do me a favor. Michael is having a really hard time with our going on tour. He thinks I'm going to die or something because he won't be there to protect me. I told him Kai would watch over me, but that just made him more irritable. So if you could kind of reassure him, and spend some time with him while I'm gone so he doesn't hole up in his room, that would be really cool of you."

I felt my face get hot. "I hate to admit it, but I'm not much better off than Michael. Truth is, I'm mostly worried that he's going to meet someone out there on the road and forget about me. Pretty stupid, huh?"

She arched her perfect eyebrows at me. "Well, yeah. Kai is the last person in the world who would cheat on you. I can't believe you don't know that."

"Part of me does. But sometimes I just freak out."

"Don't worry. We'll keep an eye on each other's guys and not let anything happen to either of them. Pinkie swear, sister?" She held out her pinkie and flashed me her beautiful smile.

I linked my pinkie with hers. "Pinkie swear." I held her gaze for a moment, and once again, I didn't feel anything other than friendship and warmth coming from her. I knew she'd take care of Kai, and I vowed to myself that I was going to keep Michael from wallowing in despair, even if it killed me.

As I was walking back up to the apartment, my phone buzzed in my pocket. "Hi Mom, how are things?"

"Not great. Laurel is a mess. Is there any chance you could come up this weekend? I think if the three of us could spend some time together it would really help her."

"Sure," I said, instantly feeling guilty. I had just promised Marlowe I'd look after Michael, and here I was leaving town on his first weekend without her. But then that gave me an idea. "Mom, I need to sort something out. I'll call you back." I hung up and hurried into our apartment, where I found Rebecca washing dishes. "Bec! What do you think about going to San Francisco this weekend with Christoph and Michael? My mom wants me to come hang out with her and Laurel, but I think it would be great if the four of us drove up there and visited Jesse and the rest."

Rebecca frowned. "I still have a lot of homework to catch up on. And finals are in a few weeks."

"But we haven't seen the San Francisco unit in ages, and it would probably be a good idea to get Michael the hell out of town for the first weekend Marlowe's on tour. Besides, I could go for a training session with Theresa. I love John, but he's been kind of, well, distracted lately."

Rebecca shut off the water. "I know. I can't explain it, but something seems really wrong with him. I've been trying to read his feelings, but I think he's blocking them or something. Can Mentors block feelings?"

"Who knows?" I answered. "John doesn't exactly give us the full story on anything. I'm sure if and when we need to know about it, he'll tell us then and not a moment before. But I know what you mean. I haven't been able to read anything from him either, other than a vague sense of sadness."

Rebecca's eyes suddenly widened. "You don't think he's coming down with the virus, do you?"

A jolt of fear shot through me. "Oh my God! If he is, and we lose our Mentor . . . "

I followed Rebecca as she raced for the door.

Once we were in my car, Rebecca tried to call John. "There's no answer," she said anxiously as she tucked her phone in her pocket.

"We're almost there." I swung around the corner and pulled into the dojo's parking lot. It was strange to see so many cars in the lot, since we had always trained when there were no other students around. Rebecca and I hopped out of the car and walked into the dojo, automatically bowing as we entered. Class was well under way, and the students were paired up working on throws. But John was nowhere to be seen.

We approached a woman who was walking among the students, advising them on their techniques. Rebecca and I bowed to her. "Excuse me," Rebecca began, "but can you tell us where John is? We're private students of his and are having trouble reaching him."

She bowed in return. "He's not here. He left a message yesterday that he was going to be out for a few days and that the black belts should teach his classes."

Rebecca and I exchanged glances. "Did he say where he went? Or when he'd be back?" I asked.

"No, just that he had personal business to take care of."

We thanked her and left the dojo. As soon as we got to the parking lot, Rebecca put her arms around my shoulders. "Recon," she whispered.

I disappeared and lifted into the air, Rebecca clinging tightly to me as I flew us over the parking lot and down the bamboo path to John's house. We circled the perimeter, peering in the windows, searching for some clue to where he went. But everything looked as it always did: spotlessly clean and tidy.

"Damn him," I hissed. "Why can't he act like a normal bachelor and leave crap lying all over the place?"

"I don't understand this," Rebecca whispered. "Why would he leave and not tell any of us?"

I flew to a window and pushed up on it, but it wouldn't budge. I tried another and another, but everything was locked up tight. I started circling higher, flying out over the avocado orchard that stretched behind John's house. I remembered not too long ago sitting under the avocado tree in his patio as he counseled me on my relationship with Kai. He had told me about how he'd cheated on his wife all those years ago, and that he hadn't dated anyone since. I realize I knew so little about this man. Why hadn't I bothered to get to know him better?

Just then, a white, fluttering object in the orchard caught my eye. Curious, I turned and flew toward it. "What is it?" Rebecca asked.

"It's a piece of paper," I said as we got closer.

"I wonder . . . " Rebecca began, but my sharp eyes had already read the words scrawled on the page.

## Deimos is ~

"Deimos is? Deimos is what?" I demanded as I swooped down and picked up the paper. I handed it to Rebecca, who read it in silence.

"John's in trouble," she said quietly. "He must not have had time to finish the note."

"Gee, you think? Or maybe he's just being John and we need to figure it out for ourselves!" I spat. "Damn it! Why couldn't he have put the important part of the sentence first? The name of a city, for example? Or better yet, who the hell we're actually supposed to be looking for!"

As my rage intensified, I felt fire gathering in my core, but a moment later a soft coolness flowed out of Rebecca's hands, quenching the fireball that was about to erupt. I touched down in the orchard and we became visible again. I sank to the ground, angry tears stinging the corners of my eyes. "We're screwed, Bec. We are so, so screwed. Deimos has John, and the only clue we have is this completely useless note. What the hell are we going to do?"

"I guess there's no choice now but to go see Theresa this weekend," she replied. She walked slowly through the trees as she called Christoph to tell him the news. I lay back on the ground and took deep breaths, trying to clear my head. Deimos had John. Kenji's parents were dying. Kai was going on tour. Laurel was a train wreck. I was barely passing my classes. *Deimos had John . . .*

I got to my feet and brushed the leaves off my pants. If Deimos really did abduct John, it was almost certainly to get to me. Which meant that I should expect a call any day now about a trade: my life for his. I was surprised at how calm I felt at this revelation, but then again, this meant that all these months and months of waiting and wondering were going to be over, that I was finally going to find out who Deimos was and face him. The anxiety had been slowly driving me crazy, and I noticed a surge of strength at the idea that the end to all of this was in sight. Even though there was a good chance I would not survive it.

## Chapter Twenty-Two: The Rift

"But you just got here!" Mom complained. "Can't it wait?"

"We're just going to have a meeting, and then I'll come back and we can watch movies. I promise."

"Ashlyn," she said in a lowered voice. "Your sister really needs us right now. Can't you go later?"

"I'll only be a couple hours."

She frowned at me. "Something's changed, hasn't it? What's going on?"

"Mom, it's all fine. We just need to sync up with the other unit and go over our next steps. Don't worry, okay?" I kissed her and left her apartment, the sound of her muttering to herself still audible after I shut the door.

"How did she take it?" Christoph asked.

"She knows something's up, but there's no way I'm telling her anything. Not yet."

"Can we please get going?" Michael grumbled.

I put the car in gear and sped to the Bay Bridge. As the city skyline rose up to meet us, a wave of sadness washed over me. I wondered how many times I'd see this view again. Rebecca reached over and put her hand on mine. "We'll take it one day at a time," she said softly.

I tried to smile. "Right. One day at a time."

"However many she has left," Michael added. A moment later the sound of Christoph punching Michael brought a true smile to my face. I was ready to kill Michael. He had sulked the entire ride north, alternating between scowling out the window in silence and making shitty comments. When we stopped for gas, Rebecca had tried to explain that he was really worried about both Marlowe and me, but I didn't have the time or patience to deal with Michael's feelings. I had to prepare myself for what was coming. And the worst part was that Kai hadn't answered any of my texts since that morning. I knew he was busy, since this was only the second day of their tour, and they had a gig in Phoenix that night. But it annoyed me that he hadn't taken a moment to text me when he knew how stressed out I was.

When Theresa opened the door, I noticed that she looked very tired, but that didn't seem to dampen her crankiness.

"You made it," she snapped. "Let's get started." We followed her into her living room, where Jesse, Paul, Raina, and Claire were already assembled. I quickly exchanged hugs with all of them and then settled down next to Jesse on the sofa.

"She's on fire," he whispered. "Just nod and smile and do whatever the hell she says."

"Kenji, are you there?" Theresa asked in a strained voice. I turned and noticed a video chat window was open on her large television screen. A moment later Kenji appeared and put on a headset.

"Sorry," he said as he adjusted the microphone. "I'm back." He looked about five years older than the last time I saw him, but this time there was a gleam in his eye.

Theresa gave him a curt nod. "Before we talk about John, Kenji has some good news for us. For a change."

Kenji beamed. "The cure is working. My mom recognized me today for the first time, and Dad looks like he's starting to come around, too."

We burst into cheers, hugging and giving each other high fives. "Kenji, that's awesome!" I said.

"I've shared what I have with the rest of the team here, and they're going to give it to a small set of patients. If it works, SymLife is going to go into production with it immediately. Oh, and they offered me a job."

"That's such great news," Claire said. "I'm so proud of you, Kenji."

"It's very good news," Theresa agreed. "That at least slows Deimos down."

"You think Deimos is behind this after all?" Rebecca asked.

"Now that John has disappeared, yes."

A quiet settled over the room as the weight of his disappearance hit us once again. "If only he'd had time to write something useful on that note," Michael said.

Theresa stared hard at him. "Useful? That note was a wealth of information. We know that Deimos is the reason that John is gone, and we don't have to waste time speculating on the cause of his disappearance. We also know that if Deimos is desperate enough to kidnap John, he feels that we are a significant threat, which means he has a weakness. Our mission is to find out what it is and exploit it."

"It has something to do with Ashlyn," Raina said. "That's pretty obvious."

"Why?" Christoph asked. "He kidnapped John, not Ashlyn."

"As bait," I explained. "And he infected me, not John."

Christoph shook his head. "I don't understand that part. If he wanted to get to Ashlyn, why not just kidnap her? Why infect her and then kidnap John?"

"This is all a complete waste of time," Michael said, getting to his feet. "We don't know who Deimos is, and until we do, there's not a damn thing we can do except sit around here like idiots."

"Sit down!" Theresa shouted. Michael glared at her, but he sat slowly back into his chair. "You are a part of this mission, whether you like it or not, and you *will* help us define our strategy." She turned to me. "Ashlyn, have you met anyone out of the ordinary lately? Come in contact with someone or something unusual?"

I shook my head. "No, nothing out of the ordinary."

"Be on the lookout every second for the slightest oddity," she ordered.

"Oh good, make her even more paranoid," Jesse said under his breath.

"And the rest of you have to be on the lookout as well. Because chances are, Deimos isn't going to stop with John."

Claire's eyes got wide. "What do you mean?

"He will try to kidnap more of us. It's what I would do if I were him." She shook her head. "You all need to start thinking like the enemy so you can anticipate his next move. We cannot keep waiting for him. Remember your training. Think about what he's been doing, what he's trying to do. If you were trying to spread evil, how would you go about it? If you wanted to get to Ashlyn, what would you do?"

"Kai," Rebecca said softly. My heart started hammering in my chest and I jumped to my feet, about to race for the door.

Michael grabbed my arm. "Relax. If he could take Kai, he would have done it already. Kai has special protection as our Keeper."

"And John doesn't?" I asked breathlessly. "How can you be so sure?"

Michael opened his mouth, apparently about to argue, when his phone rang. He yanked it out of his pocket and his face immediately softened. He put the phone to his ear as he walked out of the room. I could tell from his tone of voice that it was Marlowe.

"Michael is right," Theresa said. "Kai and Paul are our Keepers and are safe. But the rest of you aren't. And neither is your family, Ashlyn." Before I could run out the door, she quickly added, "Which is why I have already taken steps to protect them. I've hired security to keep watch on them."

"You think security guards are going to be a match for Deimos?" I shrieked.

"These are no ordinary security guards," she replied. "Your family will be fine. Trust me."

I sank into the sofa. This was my worst nightmare. Deimos was after my family. Claire, who was sitting on the other side of Jesse, reached across and placed her hand on my arm. Calm flowed through me, quieting most of my anxiety, but images of my family being abducted wouldn't stop swirling through my mind. I took deep breaths, trying to concentrate on what the others were saying.

Just at that moment, Michael came back into the room. His face was ashen. "What is it?" I asked.

He just stared at me for several moments before he finally found his voice. "It's Kai. He's missing."

I jumped to my feet. "What do you mean?"

"Marlowe said he didn't show up to the sound check for their gig. The last time they saw him was at breakfast. That was eight hours ago."

As I felt the room swaying, Jesse came over and put his arms around me, helping me sit back down on the sofa. "We don't know that he's been abducted," Theresa said. Her voice was like nails on a blackboard. "We need to stay calm."

Raina suddenly stood and glared at Theresa. "Okay, that's it. Deimos has now taken both John and Kai, but he hasn't made any demands. You say he's going to abduct more of us, but we don't know how he's going to go about it. Basically, we don't know anything, and you're asking us to sit here and try to figure it out, as if we could get inside his head. But we don't know who he is. So how exactly are we supposed to do that?"

"You are Soterians," Theresa answered icily. "You are supposed to be able to find the answers yourselves."

"Yeah, well John and Kai weren't supposed to get abducted, either," Raina spat. "I have actual work to do. If you guys get any great ideas, give me a call. Jesse, I suggest you keep an eye on Paul."

"Come back here!" Theresa snapped, but Raina simply shook her head and continued walking to the door. Michael stood and without another word followed her out. Everyone else sat perfectly still, hardly daring to breathe as Theresa's face turned angrier and uglier than I'd ever seen it. Rebecca finally sighed and got to her feet.

"I think they have a point, Theresa. Sitting here speculating isn't going to solve anything. We have no choice but to try to protect ourselves as we wait for his next move."

It took Theresa about two seconds to stride over to Rebecca, her hand raised as if she were going to strike her. But if that was her intention, we never had a chance to find out, because suddenly there was a flash, and Theresa was flat on her back with Christoph on top of her pinning her arms to the floor, a murderous expression on his face. Claire shrieked, and Jesse flew over to Christoph to pull him off. Rebecca was shouting in Christoph's ear to let Theresa go. Paul just sat looking stunned.

I felt a strange mix of what felt like fire and ice flow through my veins. I floated into the air, vaguely aware of the sensation of wind whipping around me, and watched the chaos below me as my best friends, my tribe, fought as if they were mortal enemies. I couldn't stand it one second longer. Deimos was tearing us apart and endangering the rest of the Soterians, and all because he wanted to get to me.

I flew over and plucked Christoph off Theresa as if he were no heavier than a doll, heaving him into the grand piano. Everyone dived for cover as the piano exploded, black splinters and ivory raining through the air. Rebecca screamed, and then everyone was quiet as I hovered in the middle of Theresa's living room. I was vaguely aware in that moment of all her beautiful things, her impeccable taste and money, and how none of it could do a damn thing to help us. Only one thing could.

"You are all useless!" I spat. "I am done with all of you. ALL OF YOU!" I screamed as Jesse started to fly toward me. He stopped mid-air, a look of shock and pain frozen on his face as I continued. "From this moment on, I work alone. I am going to find Deimos myself and kill him, and then I'm never going to see any of you ever again. And maybe, if I'm really lucky, I can forget that any of you ever existed in the first place." And with an angry glance at Rebecca, who was looking at me as if I were Deimos himself, I streaked toward the window, tucked my head a second before impact, and smashed through the glass and out into the chilly San Francisco night.

* * *

My brain felt like it was on fire as I streaked through the sky. I was pretty sure I'd done the right thing; the pull was stronger than any I'd ever felt. But the memory of the look on their faces as I abandoned them haunted me. Did Rebecca know? Or was she too shocked in the moment by my actions to pick up on what I was trying to tell her through my feelings? There was no way to find out now. I'd simply have to have faith that she knew me well enough to have seen through my charade.

As I continued south, the pull grew stronger, until at last I found myself flying over a large cemetery. I touched down softly on the grass between the tombstones, wondering why we were meeting here of all places. I stayed invisible even though I knew there wasn't any point.

She was standing in front of a very old grave, the silver moonlight reflecting off her long hair. Her shoulders slightly drooped, and in spite of her jeans and black hoodie sweatshirt, she looked much, much older than a teenager. I approached her quietly, and she glanced at me.

"What's your name?" she asked. "I'm assuming it's not actually Tinkerbell."

"I'm Ashlyn. You're Willow, right? Your sister mentioned your name when I flew into your hotel room."

She nodded. "She talked about you all through Germany. I thought my parents were going to have her committed."

"How come you can see me?"

She shrugged. "I don't know. But I have a connection with anything that flies. Birds, butterflies, ghosts. I learned not to ask questions."

"Why is that?"

She looked hard at me. "Because otherwise I end up back on the mental ward." She held my gaze for a second and then turned back to the grave. "This is where my great-great-great-grandmother is buried. She came to San Francisco to start a new life. Too bad plenty of people here also hated women with powers. Her poor husband was left to raise their baby daughter alone. He's buried there, next to her." Willow touched the tombstone with her finger tips. "She's always comforted me."

"Does she talk to you?" I asked. My voice sounded hoarse, like I'd been screaming.

Willow shook her head. "Not in words. Just in feelings. I knew I had to come tonight."

I was silent for a moment. "Why are we here, Willow?"

She closed her eyes and took a deep breath. "There's something deeply wrong. I've been feeling a strong evil growing over the last couple of years, but it's gotten especially bad since we got home from Germany. Finally tonight I knew you were coming and that I had to help you. I'm supposed to take you to it."

I swallowed hard. "Okay, I'm ready. I'll answer all the questions I can on the way." I turned around, and she climbed onto my back as if she'd done it every day of her life. She felt light and frail, and a powerful sense of protectiveness washed over me. I turned and glanced at the graves as I prepared to take flight. I was startled for only a moment as I read the names.

Ashlyn and Kai.

I was beginning to wonder whether anything was going to be truly surprising ever again. "Don't worry," I whispered to the graves as we sailed into the air. "I'll take care of your granddaughter. Just please, please help me find Kai and John."

## Chapter Twenty-Three: Willow

"So you let him go on tour? Even though Deimos was after you?" Willow asked.

"I know. If I'd known how dangerous things were going to become, I never would have. Trust me. Pretty much nothing matters more to me than Kai."

"Do you really think Theresa's security can protect your family?"

I bit my lip. "I just have to trust her on that one. I don't have a choice. I can't be everywhere at once." I looked down at the rolling fields glowing in the moonlight of the Napa valley. "Full moon tonight. I hope that works in our favor somehow."

"It should, unless Deimos can see you even when you're invisible."

I hadn't thought about that. At least I knew my fireball power was going to work. Only Alchemists had that power, after all, and Soterians became Alchemists specifically to fight Deimos. The trouble was, I didn't know exactly how my Alchemist powers were going to help, since Deimos couldn't be destroyed.

We flew farther north, until finally Willow pointed to a sprawling building nestled at the base of the foothills, with vineyards stretching out all around it. It looked like a white palace constructed of ancient stone, with tall columns reaching toward the heavens. It was as if a temple had been taken from Greece and dropped here in the middle of the wine country. It looked out of place compared to the many Spanish-style buildings that were popular in the area.

"That's the place," Willow said. "Deimos is there."

"Are you absolutely sure?" Now that we were here, I started to feel completely panicked. I had no idea what to do next. I couldn't just march in there and start throwing fireballs. But I could feel the pull, and I knew she was right.

Deimos was there.

And so was Kai.

I headed toward the building, but Willow tapped me on the shoulder. "Look, over there on that ridge." I followed where she was pointing and saw that high up on the ridge to the right was what looked like a large boulder with a flame coming out its top. "We should go check it out."

"Okay, but I'm keeping my distance as long as you're with me. This is just recon for now."

I made my way toward the ridge as the cold evening wind whipped my hair across my face. Willow clung a little more tightly to me. My senses were all on high alert, and my hearing and vision seemed to be more acute than ever before. I felt like all my powers were at their maximum. I almost felt ready to face what was next.

As we approached the ridge, I heard a muffled sound. I peered through the darkness, trying to identify the source, but I couldn't spot anything. "There's a sound. I think it's coming from beyond the fire," I whispered to Willow. "I'm going to circle around." I made a wide arc, scanning the area for any sign of movement or sign of life. The pull was incredibly strong now, and it took all my will not to speed straight toward the fire.

We finally reached the ridge. I squinted past the large bonfire, which was burning brightly in a stone pit, and saw a shape lying motionless on the ground. My heart thumped loudly in my chest. I was worried about going in with Willow still on my back, but I couldn't just leave the person there. What if it was Kai?

I sped back down into the valley and touched down quietly. "Hop off," I instructed Willow.

"What are you going to do?" she asked as she stepped lightly to the ground.

"There's someone up there. I need to check it out. Walk toward the road but stay as hidden as you can. Pull your hoodie up over your hair so you'll be less conspicuous. If I don't come back for you, walk to the gas station we passed about a mile down the road and get a cab. Here's some money," I said, handing her all the cash I had in my wallet. "But I should be right back." I smiled weakly at her.

"Probably not," she said. "But good luck, Ashlyn. I hope you find Kai."

I reached out and gave her a quick hug, then disappeared and sped through the air back toward the bonfire. I kept scanning the landscape for any sign of enemies, but the night was completely still. I circled around toward the back of the bonfire again, slowing down as I got closer. The shape lying on the ground now seemed to be moving slightly. Slowly, I flew closer and closer, looking all around for any sign of Deimos. A tiny glimmer of light caught my eye, and I spotted a fine web of filaments, barely visible in the bright moonlight, stretched above the figure on the ground. I thought back to our very first training exercise with John and Theresa, when Rebecca had projected the image of an owl in front of us as

211

we tripped the filaments in a window. It seemed like a thousand years ago.

I landed softly and walked carefully under the filaments, grateful for all the training John had given me on stealth. I still couldn't walk silently on rice paper, but on the dirt I was noiseless.

I crept forward until I could reach out and touch him.

Kai.

He was lying on the ground, his feet and hands bound with zip ties. I pulled the cloth gag out of his mouth, and his eyes snapped open and darted wildly around.

"Ashlyn! Is that you? Get out of here, it's --"

But before he could say another word, I heard a zing! zing! zing! as darts whizzed past me. I slammed down on top of him, keeping my head as low as I could as I grabbed my pocket knife out of my back pocket and cut through his zip ties. I shoved my arms around him and quickly flipped over onto my back, pulling him on top of me. "Get ready," I whispered, hoping he'd hear me above the shouts of what sounded like a dozen men coming toward us. After a few seconds, the darts stopped, and I exploded upward into the night sky, Kai's arms wrapped tightly around me as we burst through the web of filaments. More darts whizzed through the air below us, barely missing us. One was so close I felt it go through my hair. I flew upside down with Kai on top of me until we were out over the valley again, where I touched down with us standing up, holding each other so tightly I thought we'd break each other's ribs.

"Oh my God, Kai, are you okay? What happened?" I asked.

He pulled back. "I'm fine," he said breathlessly. "But there's no time to explain. We have to get out of here before--"

At that moment, the night was filled with the sound of barking. "Quick, hop on!" I turned my back to Kai, and the second I felt his arms around me I took to the skies again. But a few seconds later, a dart whizzed past my ear. "Damnit!" I shot straight up, until I was sure I was above the line of fire. I looked down and saw dogs and people racing from all directions toward the spot where we'd just been standing. Hoping I was high enough, I flew toward the road, searching anxiously for Willow. "She can't have gotten that far," I muttered. "Come on, come on, where are you?" Suddenly, I saw a black figure racing toward the road, and to my horror, I saw that she was being chased by a dog. I made a beeline for her, tears streaming from my eyes as the cold wind tore at my face. But right before I reached her, the dog yelped and sped in the other direction, and a second later I saw that it was being dive-bombed by dozens of bats who were chasing it back toward the middle of the valley. I swooped down and grabbed Willow, who let out a shriek of surprise as we sailed back up into the air and started flying south.

"Willow, it's us! I found Kai, he's on my back!" I felt her go limp with relief. But as I was speaking I noticed my arms were getting very weak, and I was losing altitude.

"What's wrong?" Kai asked.

"I don't know!" I said. "I'm drained. I can't keep going." I touched down next to the road, barely able to hold onto Willow long enough for her to tumble down into the grass. I sank to the ground and reached up into my hair to scratch the annoying itch that I hadn't realized had been bugging me for several minutes.

I pulled the dart out of my hair and felt where it had nicked my scalp.

My eyes started to feel heavy, and my heart was pounding. It sounded like soft galloping.

"A dog is coming!" Willow yelled. I looked up and saw a little white dog running toward us. It was almost laughable how serious such a stupid little dog looked, like it was on the most important mission of its life. But something was gnawing at the back of my mind. I'd seen that dog before. Wasn't its name . . . Carrie?

Just before I lost consciousness, I gasped as I finally realized who Deimos was.

## Chapter Twenty-Four: Revelations

"Wake up, sleepy head. Wake up."

"Mom," I groaned. "It's early. Let me sleep a bit longer."

A moment later, I was stunned by a sharp slap across my face. I blinked several times and tried to focus, but my eyes were having trouble working together. Slowly, I was able to take in the scene around me.

It was straight out of my nightmares.

I was sitting in a dimly lit room, my hands tied to the arms of my chair. It looked like it could be a barn or a garage. John, Raina, Michael, and Kai were standing against the wall, their arms tied behind their backs, while armed guards pointed guns at their heads. I quickly took inventory. No Empaths or Sentries, but no Willow, either. I prayed she got away as I looked up into the face of the person who had slapped me.

"Hello, Helen," I said, hoping I sounded braver than I felt. "Or should I say Deimos? Speaking of which, Carrie is a pretty lame nickname. So, how are things?" I forced myself to hold her gaze, even as my brain spun in circles trying to make sense of it all. Helen Lawson, the one we all thought was just a shallow, social-climbing gold digger, was the ultimate source of evil? And that stupid little dog of hers was Cerberos the hell hound? It was all so unfathomable.

She chuckled softly. "Never been better, thanks to you. And thanks to your ridiculously simple-minded Mentor." She walked over and stroked him gently on the cheek, and he looked away in disgust. "I love incarnating as a woman. Men are so very easy to manipulate. Poor John here only needed a bit of flirting, a few torrid nights, and a new motorcycle, of all things, before he was wrapped around my finger and throwing you all under the bus."

I felt like a knife had been stuck through my stomach. "Yes, Ashlyn. Your beloved guru, the ever-so-wise and powerful John Gordon, is nothing but a man after all. A man with an ego that can be used to control him. Just like everyone else."

I turned and looked at John. He was staring straight down, not making eye contact with anyone. I felt shock and then anger welling up inside of me. How could he have been so stupid? How could he have even gotten involved with her in the first place? She was a married woman who acted like a brainless twit. Was that what men really wanted? Deimos was right: in the end, we are all just human. I looked over at Michael and Raina, who were glaring at John like they wanted to kill him, and Kai, who just looked sad.

"Let them go," I said. "This is between you and me."

"You're right about that," she purred. "This is between you and me. But no, I'm not going to let them go. I need them to convince you to do the right thing and give me what I need." She nodded at the guard next to John. A second later, John cried out as the guard pistol-whipped him. He blinked in pain as blood began spurting out of his nose.

"Jesus!" I screamed. "What the hell are you doing?"

"Does that upset you?" she asked softly. "Funny, it doesn't do a thing to me. Neither will this." She nodded to the guard next to Raina, who sank his fist into her stomach with a punch so hard she doubled over and threw up.

"Stop it!" I shouted. "Tell me what you want!"

"Don't do anything that monster says," Michael said. The guard next to him reached back with his pistol to hit him. Before I knew what I was doing, a fireball shot out of me and hit the guard full in the back, knocking him into Michael before he fell to the ground screaming. His shirt was in flames, and he rolled over and over to extinguish the fire. Another guard pointed his gun at me and fired, but the bullet fell harmlessly to the ground. I felt fire building in my core again.

"Ashlyn, no!" John called. "You must not kill anyone!"

Breathing hard, I forced the fire to back down. I had never felt so much hatred in my life. I wanted to kill Deimos. Hell, I wanted to kill John for getting us into this mess. I was furious with Michael and Raina for walking out of the meeting. If they'd stayed with the others, if they hadn't turned their backs on the Soterians, they probably wouldn't have been captured.

"Oh, it gets better," Deimos said as if she were reading my thoughts. "Do you know how Kai got caught? His devotion to you is certainly strong, but every man has his weakness, and he's no exception." I stared in disbelief at Kai, who was glaring at Deimos with a cold, hard expression. "Of course, in this case, his devotion to you *is* his weakness. No matter how many beautiful women I sent his way, he simply wouldn't betray you. So finally I decided to take a different approach. I must say that the record contract was a stroke of genius. Sending him out on the road so you were apart made it so easy to play on his fears. I simply showed up, pretending to be in Phoenix for an art show. I told him that you were showing signs of getting ill again, and that I thought you needed to be with him. He couldn't leave the tour, so I suggested I fly you out to meet him in Phoenix, and when I asked if you were on a mission, pretending to be in your confidence, he said yes. And just like that, he broke his vow as a Keeper, his protection was gone, and he was mine."

I closed my eyes in disbelief. This couldn't be happening.

"The problem was that I still couldn't safely capture you. The protection of the Soterians is too strong. But when you turned your back on your units today and smashed through Theresa's lovely plate-glass window, I knew I had you." She smiled. "So you see? You've lost, Ashlyn. The only thing you can do now is give me what I want and save the lives of your units and your families."

"What exactly is it that you want?" I asked hoarsely.

"I love this body," she said, looking down at her tall, lithe frame. "It's so powerful. But human bodies are weak, and my, shall we say, *personality* weakens them even further. There's a particular virus that significantly saps my powers, and once it infects my body, I have to find another host. But soon I'll be immune, thanks to you."

My head swam. "The virus? You don't mean . . . "

"Yes. It occurred to me that with your powers, you might be able to fight it off and develop the antibodies for it. As usual, I was right."

"But why didn't you just get the antibodies, then? Why do you need me?"

"She's not just after the antibodies," John croaked. His nose was purple and swollen now. "She thinks if she takes your blood regularly, she can inoculate herself against Alchemists."

John's guard raised his pistol again, but I shot a fireball at him, stopping just short of hitting him with it and instead letting it hover between him and John. "Touch him again and you die. I mean it."

Deimos raised her hand. "Guards, leave us. And take him out of here," she said, pointing to the guard who still lay moaning on the floor. The men glanced anxiously at me as they filed out. I extinguished the fireball and looked hard at Deimos.

"You can't win," I said. "If you hurt anyone I love, my heart will close, and my powers will fade. My blood will be useless to you."

She nodded. "I'm aware of that. Which is why you will do this willingly."

"And why in the hell would I do that?"

She walked closer to me and looked deeply into my eyes, mesmerizing me. "Because of everything I'm going to offer you and the people you love. Kai is going to be successful beyond his wildest dreams. Imagine what your father will say when Kai is making more money than he ever did. You'll be able to get married, live wherever you want, with everyone's blessing. Michael will make a name for himself as a political analyst and earn the respect of his family, his friends, and people all over the world. Marlowe's career as a musician and her life with Michael will bring her greater happiness than she ever thought possible. And you can do that for her. Raina will run the best extreme sports competition the world has ever seen, and her skate shop will be legendary. John will open martial arts schools and train people all over the world. Christoph will get to stay in the United States and live happily ever after with Rebecca, who will go to Harvard Medical School and have a brilliant career." She bent over, rested her hands on the arms of my chair, and looked even

219

more deeply into my eyes. "Your mom will meet a wonderful man who will adore her and make her happy. The list goes on and on. Think of all the happiness you'll bring everyone. How can that be wrong?"

I held her gaze, seeing all the wonderful dreams she was promising as if they were already happening. The longing I felt to make those dreams happen for everyone I loved was so intense that the corners of my eyes prickled with tears.

I sighed. "You're right. I can't turn my back on the opportunity to create so much happiness for the people I love. Which is why I am going to make sure you NEVER RISE AGAIN."

Deimos narrowed her eyes and was about to speak when a sound behind her caught her attention. She whirled around, but Raina's leg was already in motion. The kick made a cracking sound as it connected with her head, and Deimos fell to the ground, unconscious.

"Leave me out of your plans, bitch," Raina spat as she hovered over Deimos' crumpled form. Michael quickly rolled her on her stomach and tied her hands behind her back.

Kai raced over and threw his arms around me. "Jesse, get Ashlyn out of this," he barked. Jesse reappeared and walked over to me with his usual smirk.

"Theresa's livid," Jesse said. "Couldn't you have made a less dramatic exit? That window is going to cost a fortune to replace." He cut the zip ties with his knife and I rubbed my wrists.

"I had to make it look like I'd completely flipped out. I'm just glad Rebecca knew what I really meant."

He looked incensed. "Hey, I'm the one who figured it out first. I mean, who could possibly never want to see me again?"

"Me, if you don't shut up. But I have to admit, I've never been so happy to see anyone as I was a minute ago when you drifted in." He made duck lips at me, and I got up and walked over to John. Rebecca and Claire were huddled with him on the floor, and his nose was almost back to normal. "We've only got a few minutes before she comes around, so I'll make this fast. I know nobody can ever punish you more than you're already punishing yourself, John, and I forgive you. We are human. All of us," I said, glancing around. "And being human and flawed is what makes us perfect." I leaned down and kissed him on the cheek. "All of you clear out now."

"No way," Raina said. "We're staying and seeing this through."

I shook my head. "You can't. I have to do this alone."

"She's right," John said. "We have to go."

Kai took my hand. "Are you absolutely sure?"

"Yes," I said. "Don't worry. I think I finally know what I have to do." I kissed him and watched him walk out with Rebecca, who gave me a sad smile. We'd been communicating furiously through our feelings for the last hour. There was nothing left to say out loud.

Michael approached me. "You don't actually have any fucking idea what you're going to do, do you?"

I smiled. "Take care of Marlowe, Michael. She loves you."

He looked searchingly at me, then took my face in my hands and kissed me gently, making my knees go weak. He gave me one last smoldering glance and walked out the door.

I turned and looked at Deimos, who was starting to stir. Well, this was it. After all my training, searching, and waiting, I was finally face-to-face with Deimos. The last battle was here.

And I still didn't know how to defeat her.

I looked at her golden hair and perfect body. She chose to incarnate as someone rich and powerful who could easily manipulate people. She was trying to create a perfect host, one who was immune to viruses, to weaknesses. For a second, I envied her as I imagined what it would be like to be perfect, never having to worry whether I was good enough or that Kai would grow weary of my flaws. Then again, Kai always said he didn't want me to be "perfect," that he loved me just as I was. And that's when it hit me: maybe what he was trying to say was that he loved me not *in spite* of my flaws but *because* of them. Maybe love thrives on imperfection, because it's what makes us unique, and it's what makes us human.

Deimos opened her eyes, and it was if the world had shifted 180 degrees. Suddenly I truly understood what love was, and how the world worked. It all made sense. All of it. The reason that channeling both good and evil gave me such amazing powers was because I wasn't trying to keep one and push the other away—I was simply accepting whatever came in, without judgment, with total openness, whether it was fear, anger, sorrow, or joy. Kai's love was not the key to my powers—the key was my willingness to open my heart completely, to be vulnerable, and to show him my imperfections no matter how much that exposed me to getting hurt. My love for Kai was so strong, I couldn't help but be open to him, and in the process, to everything else. And when I tried to control it, to shut out the possibility of pain and loss, and I closed my heart and chose to sink into fear instead, that's when my powers faded. Love was the key to my powers, but that love was simply a choice made by me. Kai wasn't actually required to trigger it—he just taught me how to open the door.

And in that moment, all judgment dropped away, and I felt complete and total love for everyone around me. For

John, the wonderful and intelligent and weak man that he was. For Raina, for her fierce, hard spirit that kept us alive while keeping her alone. For Michael, who had overcome so many demons and learned to open his heart, just as I had. And for the first time, I felt love and total acceptance of myself, not in spite of my imperfections, but because of them.

I watched Deimos slowly sit up with a fire blazing in her eyes, breaking the zip ties like they were mere threads. I found it funny that it took the ultimate source of evil to teach me about love. I felt a wave of bliss as gratitude for every single person in my life spilled out of me. For my mom, for her incredible support. For my dad, for his indomitable will that kept me pushing past my limits. For Kelly, for the love she and Kai shared once, and for being a good friend to Tracy. Even for the teacher in high school who hated me and gave me an F in math, I felt gratitude and love for him simply because he was part of the fabric of my life. My short, meaningless life.

"Thank you," I said to Deimos, my voice sounding pure and resonant, almost musical. I was so happy I still had a voice, for however long. "Thank you for what you've shown me. I'm not afraid anymore."

I reached out with my feelings and felt the others retreating into the night, and I wanted to put my arms around every one of them, to feel their warmth against my body one last time, to thank them for walking this incredible journey with me. I had no idea what would happen in the next moment, but it didn't matter. I was alive for now, fully alive, for the first time in my life. For just that one moment, my heart was fully open, and I felt connected to every single person in the world, and through that connection I poured all the love that was now flooding through me on a stream of gratitude and appreciation for the uniqueness and perfect imperfections of every living being. I felt a tiny spark of recognition coming from every corner of the globe as we all felt a moment of peace, of acceptance for ourselves and everyone else. For the briefest moment, nobody hated anyone else, and nobody hated themselves. For a tiny moment, there was no fear.

And that was when it happened. That peace I felt in each person turned into a fire that flowed back into me like lava, filling my heart and lungs and throat and finally bursting forth from every cell in my body in an explosion. I watched in slow motion as it bloomed into the biggest fireball I'd ever seen, enveloping the building in a fire so white hot that I thought the very earth below us would melt. I was only vaguely conscious of the sensation of a cool mist surrounding my body, protecting me from the impossible heat.

Deimos' eyes became very wide. She opened her mouth, but no sound came out. She began to twist and contort, and then let out a howl.

"It's okay," I said, my voice sounding like it was deep in a well. "You can never be destroyed, because as long as there are human beings, there will be fear, and therefore there will be evil, and you will rise again when evil takes over once more. But the balance has been restored. Rest, and let the world be without you for a while." She continued to twist and scream in agony, but like labor pains, this was perfect, this was natural. It was happening the way it was meant to. And I felt gratitude all over again for the perfect order of the universe that let stories run their course and heroes and villains think they're struggling against each other when they're really struggling with themselves. I marveled at the subtle, impossible working of the cosmos and the earth rotating at just the right speed. And Deimos, rising like a shadow over the earth whenever we get ahead of ourselves and forget who we are and convince ourselves that our evils aren't really all that bad anyway and that the ends justify the means and of course I'll do good things with my ill-gotten power and money, just not today.

With one last look of pure hatred, Deimos swayed and then collapsed. She looked like a wax figure thrown in a furnace, her face and limbs melting until she was no more than a puddle on the scorched concrete floor. I marveled at the peace that was still flowing through me from every corner of the earth as I watched the puddle evaporate. And then I was alone. I stood there for some time, listening to the sound of my breath and the roar of the flames, enjoying the intense heat tempered by the cool mist.

But a moment later, I heard the sound of shouts and running footsteps. It was time to come back to my life. To be Ashlyn again. I let the fireball extinguish, pulling it back into my core. The last flame flickered at the tip of my index finger, and then I was in darkness.

A moment later, I made out the shape of Rebecca running toward me, followed closely by the others.

"Ashlyn! Ashlyn, oh my God, I couldn't feel you anymore, and I thought . . ." Rebecca glanced around. "Is she gone?"

"It's over," I said. "Look." I took Rebecca's hand and wrapped it around my bruised wrist. A moment later, I pulled her hand away. The bruises had only faded slightly. She looked confused, and then the realization settled over her face. "It's going to take some getting used to, but we're going to be fine," I said as the tears started flowing freely down both our faces. "We're all going to be just fine."

## Chapter Twenty-Five: Open Arms

"I don't like this," Rebecca said as she watched Christoph climb into the fireproof suit. "Claire and I don't have enough healing even between the two of us to take care of this if someone gets hurt."

"Come on," Christoph said. "This is a brilliant idea. I've wanted to do this ever since you told me about the fire suits you wore when Ashlyn was insane."

"My powers are so weak now, I really don't think I can do much damage," I said. "Besides, we're on the beach. He can always run into the ocean if he catches fire." I took Kai's hand as I looked across Baker Beach and over the water to the Golden Gate bridge. It still amazed me how little time had passed since that night we saved it from being destroyed and I almost died. My thoughts were interrupted by the sound of Laurel's laughter, and I looked over at where she and Kenji were sitting together, talking about Japan.

"The first time I walked into a market, I said, *Moshi Moshi* to the guy behind the counter," Laurel said.

Kenji laughed. "You only say that when you're answering the phone."

"I know that *now*. He looked at me like I was crazy."

226

Kenji beamed at her and they continued sharing stories and laughing. He had flown into San Francisco the day before, and Laurel had joined us for dinner. When she heard his parents were from Japan, they discovered they had a lot in common and had been hanging out pretty much non-stop ever since. I was happy she was getting over Jason. I didn't hate him anymore. He had his own path to follow, and even though it meant he'd caused Laurel a ton of pain and he'd acted like a douchebag, there was something for her to learn from it, too.

"Is it weird for you?" Michael asked me.

"Which part?"

"Not being on the lookout for Deimos anymore."

I shook my head. "That will never stop. But the difference is that I'm not seeking to destroy her anymore. Or him. It."

"You wouldn't get the chance," he said. "No way is Deimos ever coming near you again."

"Maybe not. But if I ever feel its presence, I'll be opening my heart. As long as I can avoid fearing it, I can help keep it from rising."

Just then my mom and John walked up. "I spoke with Willow," John said. "She sounds like a normal teenager now."

"Poor girl," Mom said. "I don't wish that on anyone."

Rebecca nodded. "It's better than seeing ghosts all the time, though. I hope she gets to keep the affinity with birds."

"And bats," Kai added. "That was pretty cool."

"Let's do this!" Christoph said in a muffled voice from inside the fire suit. My mom looked horrified.

"Ashlyn! You're not serious!"

John put his arm around her. "It'll be fine, Elise." They looked at each other, and I thought I saw something pass between them in their gaze. John quickly dropped his arm and glanced around. "Anyone coming?"

I looked up and down the beach and stretched my hearing as far as I could. My senses had become so much less acute that at first I felt blind and deaf by comparison. But I was quickly getting used to my new existence. Fewer powers were a small price to pay for a lot more peace. "I think it's all clear." I walked toward Christoph, who was grinning inside the suit. "Ready?"

"Ready!" he said.

I focused on pulling all the fear I could. I felt the anxiety of students who were studying for exams. Teenage girls scrutinizing their bodies in the mirror with dismay. Children worrying about monsters under the bed. A group of drunks heckling a gay man outside a bar. I drew it all to me, mingled it with the tremendous love that was overflowing from the amazing people I was lucky enough to call friends, and felt the fire building in my core. With great effort, I shot a small stream of fire at Christoph, who started hopping around in the flames, waving his arms in glee.

"Hey, I want to try!" Jesse said, jumping to his feet.

"Wait your turn, whippersnapper!" Christoph shouted as he ran back and forth through the stream of fire like a delighted little kid playing with the hose on a summer day.

"That's it for now," I gasped. "Give me some time to recharge." I plopped down on the sand next to Rebecca as Christoph took off the hood and whooped in delight. "He really is going to be a kick-ass daycare teacher," I told her.

"What about you?" she asked.

"Me? I'm not starting a daycare."

"No, I mean what do you think you want to do? You never talk about it."

"Ah, yes, well, that's because until recently I didn't really think I had a future waiting for me. But now, I think I've finally settled on going to flight school. I'm going to be a helicopter pilot. Being able to maneuver and hover in the air again is going to be so cool."

"A helicopter pilot!" Mom shrieked. "Oh Ashlyn, why can't you pick something that won't give me a heart attack?"

"Because this way I save you from dying of boredom. Well, friends, I have to get Kai to the airport." We said our good-byes, and I walked with Kai up the beach. "I'm going to miss you like crazy," I said.

"I know. I'm sorry you can't come with me."

"Me too, but if I want to have any hope of graduating, I have to get back to school. And I might just blow up your amp again."

"That's one thing I'm definitely not going to miss," he said, giving me his adorable crooked smile.

We got into the car and headed for the airport, the San Francisco skyline shrinking behind us. I couldn't believe that my whole life was waiting for me again. That Kai and my family were alive and well. That Deimos had been defeated. And that all my goals seemed closer now than they ever had, even in that brief moment when I found myself questioning whether I shouldn't just take Deimos up on the offer to make all my dreams come true. It wasn't really that hard a decision: work to achieve your dreams the hard way, or sell your soul and have everything handed to you? Few people ever get to make that kind of a choice, but I realized that it happens all the time in much subtler ways. After what I'd seen, I knew I would never again take the easy path if it meant causing suffering to someone else or to myself down the road.

Kai took my hand and gave me that piercing look that always made me so giddy. The radio started playing the ColdPlay song I'd heard so long ago when I first left for Santa Barbara, and we sped down the highway to meet our future with open arms.

## Kai Anderson

Hey, Kai, what's your 20?

We're just pulling into Seattle.
Where are you?

About 1,000 ft up

What have I told you about
texting and flying?

Says the man who texted me a
pic of the arena during his gig.
It looked like about 60,000 of
your closest friends were there.

That was different. We were
between songs.

And I'm between clients. Don't
worry, I'll be on the ground soon.

In one piece, I hope. You still on
schedule to meet me up here?
Michael is already here, of course.

My flight leaves at 6. I'll make it.

It would have been so much cheaper
if you were an airline pilot.

It's cooler that you're married to
a helicopter pilot.
I can't wait to see you.

Me neither. You rock my world, love.

And you rock mine, Waterfall.
Fly safely.

Where's the fun in that?

Sigh. <3

# Afterword

Originally, I had intended for the Soterians series to be five books, but I realized as I was writing *Madness* that the threads were tying themselves up sooner than I'd anticipated, and the story I'd outlined for book five (which was going to be called *Equinox*) was too much of a departure from the rest of the books. And so instead of trying to squeeze out a fifth book that didn't really fit the series, I decided to cut *Equinox* and finish the series with *Madness*. (The beauty of being a self-published author is that I don't have any contractual obligations to a publisher.)

Throughout the series, I've written the stories I wanted to tell and ignored many well-meaning comments about how I could make them more marketable. I think it's fantastic when people buy my books, but I'm much more interested in getting my stories out there to readers than making money, which is why I price them as low as possible. The result is that I've attracted a surprising number of fans, and my characters, who have become family to me, have made their way into the hearts of people all over the globe.

To all of you who have read my books, written reviews, liked the Soterians Facebook page, and sent me fan mail, I am forever in your debt. Writing the Soterians series has been one of the most rewarding projects of my life, and I encourage any of you who have a story to tell to pursue your dream. Self-publishing isn't for everyone, but if you want the experience of writing something you love and getting it out there for people to enjoy, you will find it highly rewarding.

## About the Author

Jacquelyn has worked as a professional writer since 1991. She has received numerous awards for her technical writing, but creative writing has always been her passion. After writing poetry, children's stories, and screenplays, Jacquelyn embarked on The Soterians series, a series of fantasy novels for young adults. As an advocate for volunteerism and service, Jacquelyn donates 20% of her royalties to the charities listed on her Web site (www.soterians.com).

In her spare time, Jacquelyn enjoys martial arts, triathlons, skiing, playing music, and volunteering. She lives in the San Francisco Bay Area.

www.ingramcontent.com/pod-product-compliance
Lightning Source LLC
Chambersburg PA
CBHW050039180626
46810CB00002B/798